ALSO BY TRISTAN BANCKS

MAC SLATER HUNTS THE COOL

Mac Slater
vs. THE CITY

TRISTAN BANCKS

SIMON & SCHUSTER BOOKS FOR YOUNG READERS
NEW YORK   LONDON   TORONTO   SYDNEY

SIMON & SCHUSTER BOOKS FOR YOUNG READERS
An imprint of Simon & Schuster Children's Publishing Division
1230 Avenue of the Americas, New York, New York 10020

Originally published as *Mac Slater, Coolhunter 2: I Heart NY* in Australia in 2008 by
Random House Australia Pty Ltd.
Published by arrangement with Random House Australia Pty Ltd.
First U.S. edition April 2011
For information about special discounts for bulk purchases, please contact Simon &
Schuster Special Sales at 1-866-506-1949 or business@simonandschuster.com.
The Simon & Schuster Speakers Bureau can bring authors to your live event. For more
information or to book an event, contact the Simon & Schuster Speakers Bureau at
1-866-248-3049 or visit our website at www.simonspeakers.com.
Book design by Chloë Foglia
The text for this book is set in Bembo.
Manufactured in the United States of America
0311 FFG
10 9 8 7 6 5 4 3 2 1
Library of Congress Cataloging-in-Publication Data
Bancks, Tristan.
Mac Slater vs. the city / Tristan Bancks. — 1st ed.
p. cm. — (Mac Slater hunts the cool)
Summary: Mac and his reluctant friend Paul head from Australia to Manhattan to
continue their work for the Coolhunter website, and once there they discover a
group of young inventors whose work is meant to be kept top-secret.
ISBN 978-1-4169-8576-1 (hardcover)
[1. Inventions—Fiction. 2. Inventors—Fiction. 3. New York (N.Y.)—Fiction.
4. Australians—United States—Fiction. 5. Popular culture—Fiction. 6. Web
sites—Fiction.] I. Title.
II. Title: Mac Slater versus the city
PZ7.B21766Mav 2011
[Fic]—dc22
2010006858

Dedicated to you.
Hope it inspires you to create.

Special thanks to all the fine humans who helped to bring this book to page: Amber Melody, Sophie Hamley, Catherine Drayton, Nerrilee Weir, Emily Meehan, Julia Maguire, and all the amazing people at Simon & Schuster putting books in the hands of kids and teenagers everywhere.

I love where I'm from but, to me, if you're gonna go anywhere, you go to New York. Even to smell the place. That's just the way it is.

—*Mac Slater Hunts the Cool*

← Coolhunters →

Coolhunters are teens and twenty-somethings with their fingers on the pulse of the freshest, hottest ideas and innovations coming off the street. The people who recognize cool stuff way before anyone else sees it. Big companies rely on coolhunters to tell them what's up and to give feedback on shoes, clothes, and technology before they hit shelves. Coolhunters influence what we eat, wear, listen to, drive, ride, watch, and buy.

welcome to new york

The lights were blinding. Four lanes of traffic coming right at us. We jerked to a stop. I panicked and looked across to Dad—his scruffy, jet-lagged face hot white in the headlights. And he just sat there.

"Turn around! It's one way," I screamed. Dad went to flick his turn signal on but hit the wipers instead. Then he revved the engine hard, spun the wheel, and stalled. The wall of traffic coming down Broadway was about forty feet away now, horns blasting. A car in our lane sped straight toward us.

"Go!" I yelled at Dad.

"What?" Paul said, waking up in the backseat and planting his glasses back on his nose. Paul's my best friend and he's kind of a scaredy cat. He saw the traffic heading our way and let out a bloodcurdler.

Dad cranked the engine again, but it was too late. The car heading for us veered hard to the right, passing so close that our car rocked on its wheels. Then a yellow cab behind it came ripping toward us. I wanted to jump into the backseat to get away. Cars tore by, right and left. I braced myself, closing my eyes, ready for impact. There was no way the cab wasn't going to hit us.

I heard brakes slam hard, a bunch of cars shredding rubber all over Broadway. But no bang.

I opened my eyes. The cab was nose to nose with us. The driver leaned out the window and blurted all this crazy abuse in a language I couldn't quite catch. Then the insults started from people going by. Thick New York accents. And Italian, Korean, and maybe Indian and Irish.

"Get off the road."

"C'mon, man!"

"Get off the #@$%&★! road, you %$^&★@!"

After what seemed like forever, the lights changed at the next intersection and the block was suddenly empty. Dad breathed out heavily. Paul and I were mute. Then we heard a single, sharp note from a siren.

"Oh, here we go," Dad said, looking in the rearview.

"What?"

Our car was filled with red and blue light. A cop on a motorcycle cruised up next to us.

I covered my face with my hands. Paul and I were supposed to be here on our first international coolhunt, a weeklong trend-spotting mission for Coolhunters, a massive web space getting more than a million hits a day. But the trip so far hadn't been as cool as it could have been.

To get here we'd had to stop in five other cities. Paul was terrified of flying, so he sweated and freaked the whole way instead of sleeping. When we landed, Dad's and Paul's bags weren't on the luggage carousel. Then the customs guy grilled Dad about his dodgy prison record for protesting nuclear power. A security woman spent ten minutes pulling my boxers out of my bag and laying them on a table for everyone to see, including the cute girl who'd been sitting across the aisle from me on the plane. Finally, a dude gave me a Mickey Mouse stamp in my passport (Paul got Minnie) and said, "Welcome to New York."

Speed and Tony, our Coolhunters bosses, had promised to meet us when we got off the plane, but they were nowhere to be seen. We tried their phones, but they went to voice mail. We hung at the airport for two and a half hours, waiting. Around 11:30 p.m. we went to grab a cab and discovered there was a taxi strike, so we rented a car. (We got a hybrid, which was cool. Paul and I planned to invent our own biofuel some day.) But the thing is, my dad's way sketchy behind the wheel. He doesn't even own a car. Says they trash the planet. But tonight he'd said, "It's late. There won't be much traffic. We'll be fine."

Famous last words.

The cop arrived at Dad's window.

"Whaddya doin' there, sir?"

Dad fumbled for the electric window button. I don't know if he'd ever used one before. Once the window was down a crack, he said, "I've . . . I've never driven on a road with more than two lanes. I'm sorry. I'm . . ."

"It's a one-way street. Don't matter how many lanes it's got, sir. You do have to be movin' in the correct direction, however. You don't have one-way streets where you come from?"

"No," said my dad. "We don't."

It was true. Kings Bay didn't even have a traffic light.

"Well, you got about seven seconds before that traffic signal changes again, sir. I suggest you move. Have a nice night."

Motorcycle guy waited as my dad turned the key and spun the car around, tires squealing.

"That was cool," I said, grinning.

Dad shot me a dark look.

I had a habit of laughing at the wrong time, just when things were going wrong. My folks never seemed to like it much. I stuck my head out the window and sucked in a deep breath. New York smelled good. Like fumes and possibility.

We headed back down Broadway to find a place to stay. We scoured the city for an hour and finally found a room we could almost afford in a dump called the Big Apple Hotel.

But, throughout it all, no matter what was going wrong, I

couldn't wipe the smile off my face. I swear I started dreaming about this city forever ago, and somehow, the more screwed up things were, the more I loved it. We were on a weeklong mission to hunt cool in New York City. Does it get any better than that?

The Big Lemon

"Two hundred and fifty-seven dollars and thirty-seven cents, including taxes, thank you, sir."

"You don't have a standby rate or anything, do you?" my dad asked.

"No, sir. We are almost fully booked this evening, and the Big Apple is one of the best value hotels in the city."

Dad rummaged through his paper-thin brown leather wallet, then shoved a handful of greenbacks through a small opening in a cage separating us from the chirpy receptionist. His neat hair, cheery voice, and bright blue sports coat with gold buttons clashed with the surroundings. The lobby, if you could call it that, was more like a broom closet with an elevator and a snack machine. We barely fit in there. The room was lit by a flickering fluorescent light mounted on the wall. Jazz played quietly on a crackly, old-school ghetto blaster that had a ginger cat sitting on top of it.

"There you go, sir," said Happy Guy, dropping a few coins back through the slot. I grabbed them and stuck them into my little homemade New York book in my back pocket. The book was going to be our guide to the city.

"Your room key, sir. Room six-oh-six on the sixth floor. Please familiarize yourselves with the hotel's fire evacuation procedures on the back of your door. Breakfast will be—"

"Fire?" Paul whispered to me.

"It's just a precaution, sir," said Neat-Hair Guy. "Coffee and doughnuts will be available between seven thirty and eight thirty a.m."

Paul nudged me and I grinned. How American is that? Who else in the world eats doughnuts for breakfast? My mom was a raw-food freak, so all I ever got at home was a bowl of uncooked oats with homemade rice milk. Lately, she'd been making organic pine-needle smoothies. So wrong. There's a reason normal people don't drink trees.

Dad hit the elevator button. There was a groan of ancient machinery as it lumbered down the shaft. Through a barred gate we could see the old cables swing and rattle.

Paul was starting to panic. Small spaces were one of his many fears.

"Can we take the stairs?" he asked.

"No, sir," said the receptionist. "They are on the exterior of the building and are only to be used in case of fire."

The elevator arrived. It was about the size of an old phone booth. Dad wrestled with the double swinging doors and squeezed inside. I followed, backpack on.

"I can't go in there," Paul said.

"It's all right, man. It'll be okay," I said.

"I'm not coming in."

"Dude. Get in," I said sharply, then whispered, "or you can sleep down here with Gold Buttons and the cat."

The receptionist looked up. The cat meowed. Paul got into the elevator. He was allergic to cats. And to weird receptionists.

Dad's massive frame took almost every square inch of space. He plucked his arm out from behind my back, swung the doors shut, and hit number six, the top floor. Nothing happened, so he hit the button again.

"My throat's closing up," Paul said.

I clenched my teeth. This was classic Paul Porter. When the chips were down, pull out a random phobia. As Dad reached to hit the button a third time, there was a high-pitched whine and the elevator heaved us upward.

"Hey, look. Maximum load: two passengers," I said with a grin, pointing to a sticker on the wall.

Paul looked as sick as two dogs. Dad tried to act relaxed, but even his beard looked concerned. Then he farted. He often did that when he was nervous.

"Sorry. Plane food," he said.

"I'm gonna die!" Paul whined, unable to move his arms to cover his nose.

I started laughing, thinking what a bad way to die this would be. The stench was particularly foul, even by my dad's standards.

Enough to make you question vegetarianism as a lifestyle choice.

When we hit the sixth floor, the doors flung open, and we exploded into a darkened hallway. It looked like the scene of a crime, lit at the far end by a sickly yellow glow from a single bulb over room 606. Along the grimy left-hand wall were stacks of toilet paper and soft-drink boxes. The rooms were on the right-hand side. Shouting came from behind one of the doors, two men having an argument.

"Is that TV or real people?" I asked.

No one answered. I grabbed my bag and we moved quickly down to the end of the hall. Our room was next to the screamers. Great. Dad fiddled with the key, shoved open the door, and stabbed at the light switch. We stopped in our tracks. I swear it had to be the only room in New York smaller than the lobby. At home I live in a double-decker bus with my mom so, believe me, I know small.

"S'pose this is it," Dad said.

We stepped inside. The double bed sagged in the middle like a horse had been sleeping in it. I edged my way along the twelve-inch gap between the side of the bed and the wall. I peered out through the tiny uncurtained window. The view was of bricks, less than a yard away. The so-called bathroom was the size of a shower, but they'd somehow squeezed a toilet and sink in there too. And the place reeked of cigarette smoke and urine.

"This is nice," I said.

No one laughed.

"It's disgusting," Paul said. "We're leaving."

"What? To go where?" I asked him. "You want to get back in the car and look at more hotels?"

"I can't breathe in here," he said.

"It's fine," I said firmly.

"What about *them*?" Paul asked, referring to the screamers next door.

"It's just TV."

There was a massive bang, and a picture fell off the wall in our room. Someone had smashed into the other side. I swear I heard one of the dudes say, "Gimme the freakin' money." Did people really say "Gimme the freakin' money" in New York?

"It's just for tonight," Dad grunted. "We'll find somewhere else tomorrow."

"If we're still alive," I said under my breath.

The door to the next room slammed, and then someone started banging on our door.

"Help! Open up already!"

We stayed quiet. Dad flicked off the light. Should we open the door? Did this guy really need our help?

"Open up! Now!" the voice said again, more aggressive than scared.

We all stood there in the dark. Now I felt *my* throat closing up. The smell of the place melted away. Hearing was my only sense. The guy banged on our door one more time and then muttered to himself. We heard his footsteps disappear down the hall, and a minute later we heard the elevator heave to life.

Dad flicked on the light again. There was no way we were leaving the room now. We barely said a word as we got ready for bed, all lost in our own private thoughts on what might happen next. Dad and I slept head to toe in the double bed. We both rolled into the giant trench in the middle, which meant I had his crusty bunions in my face all night. Paul slept on the narrow strip of floor next to the bed. Just as well he's so skinny. He laid our only blanket down to protect himself from the filthy carpet and whined for half an hour before boring himself to sleep.

I tried to breathe deeply and sleep too, but I couldn't even close my eyes. I pulled my New York book out from under my pillow and flicked through it in the yellow glow spilling through the crack under the door. The book was filled with maps and photos I'd taped in, notes I'd jotted, and stuff printed off the web about all the things that juiced me about New York. On the cover was a chick wearing an I HEART NY T-shirt.

I shut the book and lay there listening to sirens yowling in the distance and the echo of traffic bouncing up between buildings. I tried not to think about the fact that our Coolhunters bosses had ditched us. From the beginning I'd had this feeling they were kind of sketchy.

Good Morning, ◁ America ▷

"Blood! Blood!" someone screamed.

I rolled over and fell down into the gap between the bed and the wall, onto Paul's makeshift cot.

"Blood!" came the shriek again.

My dad jumped out of bed and trod on my face on his way to the bathroom. I dragged myself up and followed him. Paul was standing there—hair like a mad professor's, bath mat around his waist—looking at all this red water pouring from the shower.

"It's not blood. It's rust!" my dad growled.

"It's blood!" Paul said.

"It's rust," I croaked. I knew. Our bus at home had rusty water too. "What'd you wake us up for?" I asked, only then really remembering where we were. I went straight to the window and looked out, searching for any sign of New Yorkness, but it was all wall.

There was a TV up high at the end of the bed, and I flipped

it on. I needed to see something to prove that we were actually here and not in some cheap dive in my hometown. An infomercial for a DVD called *You Power* flicked up on-screen. A guy with capped teeth was asking a woman in orange and black Lycra some fake questions about taking control of her life. It was cool.

"TV!" I said to Dad. He was back in bed, head under the covers.

"I didn't know they had TV here," he said.

"Ha ha. If either of my parents had a TV, I wouldn't have to come to New York to watch it."

Dad pulled the covers off his head and watched for a minute.

A whole bunch of people in tracksuits were now standing in a park with their arms in the air. They screamed, "You Power," and the ordering details hit the screen. "Call now and get this limited edition crystal mouse. You'll never see another offer like this!"

"You've really been missing out," Dad said, retreating back to his lair.

"How am I going to take a shower if it's spitting rust all over me?" Paul whined from the bathroom.

"I dunno, but hurry up," I said, unzipping my bag and grabbing some jeans. "Imaginator's waiting."

Imaginator was a massive invention fest. It was pretty much the reason Paul agreed to get on the plane. The fest promised the wildest minds on earth dishing out the latest breakthroughs in tech, cars, flying machines, clothes, phones, and everything else. We figured it'd be a one-stop shop for coolhunting and a chance for Paul and me to talk up our flying bike.

"And we've only got seven minutes till coffee and doughnuts is over," I said.

"Nuts. Why didn't you say?" Paul said, flicking off the tap and pulling his plane clothes back on.

Four minutes later, we were downstairs wearing icing-sugar mustaches and chowing our second doughnuts as we gazed out the door onto the street. Hundreds of yellow cabs ripped by. I could see a New York fire hydrant. I was a little disappointed that it wasn't spewing water with kids playing under the spray like in the pic in my book but, still, a real fire hydrant! Millions of people in suits charged by, sucking down coffee or screaming into phones. I tried to think how many times in my life I'd seen someone wearing a suit. Even real estate dudes didn't wear suits in Kings Bay.

I poured myself a coffee from the percolator. Paul grabbed another doughnut from the basket next to it. I held my nose and tried to force the coffee down my throat, just to feel like a New Yorker. Even with my nose plugged it tasted like ash and dirt. I spat it back into the cup.

"What do we do now?" Paul asked.

Speed and Tony from Coolhunters had told us they'd give us an allowance each day to live on. That was how we could afford the trip. My dad was a protester who ran a lightning farm. Not exactly a credit card kind of guy.

"Dunno," I said.

"My phone won't work, so how're they s'posed to contact us?" Paul asked. "Maybe we should see if we can change our flights home."

"Oh, here we go." I rolled my eyes.

"What?"

"You! You sound like your old lady," I said.

It had taken about thirty-seven meetings to persuade Paul's mom to let him come to New York. My ma's only worry was that we wrote off our carbon miles. At one stage it even looked like Paul's mom might chaperone. But there was no way I was having that. I was desperate to hunt cool in New York, but not that desperate.

"I'm just—"

"You're just looking for a way to get out of doing new stuff," I said. "This is our dream. We've been talking about this forever. Now, we're going upstairs, getting Dad, and going to Imaginator, just like we planned."

His eyes lit up a little.

"We'll scope the fest," I said, "so when we catch up with Speed and Tony we'll have hunted a ton of cool already."

"But—"

"We'll call home. Speed and Tony will have left a message. We'll rock on over to the real hotel—probably in a stretch Hummer—and everything will be cool beans."

Paul stared at me. He didn't believe a word I'd said. Neither did I.

"Imaginator, man. Let's do it."

Dad got out of the elevator and guzzled three black coffees. Then we hit the streets.

Lost

New York hit us like a train. Horns blared. Jackhammers juddered high above. Briefcase people charged, head down, right for us, like we weren't even there. An obese woman pushed past, attempting to walk four gigantic dogs through the crowd. Dad went over to the rental car and rubbed the meter maid's chalk mark off the tire with a wet thumb. We were on the corner of Thirty-fourth Street, with Broadway stretching away from us forever—a long, narrow canyon of concrete and glass shooting up into the sky. It was supposed to be spring, but in the shadow of the scrapers, it was freezing.

I fed a bunch of quarters into a pay phone and punched Speed's digits. Then Tony's. Both went to message, so I called home. We didn't have a phone in the bus. Mr. Kim, the owner of the arts village where we lived, always had to run down from the office with his cordless phone. It was nearly midnight at home.

The phone rang. And rang. I looked around me. There was an old guy sitting on a box playing blues guitar. He had a harmonica on a neck holder. There were a couple of college-student-looking chicks filming a mime artist who was painted red from head to toe. The phone kept ringing. A superhairy dude wearing three watches and a court jester's hat walked by, sucking a yard-long licorice rope into his mouth. I was about to hang up when I heard a voice.

"Mr. Kim? . . . Yeah, it's Mac. . . . Yeah, good. . . . Thanks. Thanks."

A bunch of quarters dropped, so Dad gave me another handful and I fed them into the phone as quickly as I could. A few minutes later I heard my mom's voice.

"Ma," I said.

Paul's ears pricked up.

"Sort of," I said. "I mean, yeah, everything's cool, but we sort of can't find the Coolhunters guys. They haven't called, have they?"

Paul stared at me hard, waiting for a response.

A massive truck groaned by. "Sorry, Ma, what'd you say?"

Paul strained to hear, mouth open.

"Oh, right," I said when she told me. I shook my head at Paul.

"This sucks!" he said. "These guys are a joke."

My dad looked semi-stressed, in his own laid-back way. He

pulled at his beard. I could tell he wanted to be home with his dogs. He was so not New York.

"No, we'll be okay. We'll find them, I'm sure—"

My last quarter dropped and the phone went dead.

"I knew they were scammers," Paul said.

"Oh, poor you. You're lost in New York. I feel so sorry for you, man."

Paul shoved me in the chest.

"These guys paid for our flights, didn't they?" I said.

"Yeah, on the worst airline in the history of earth, making us stop seventeen times on the way," Paul yelled at me over the roar of a bus.

"Why would they pay for our fares and then just strand us here? It doesn't make sense. We'll be fine. Relax."

"Well, I hope you've got plenty of money," my dad said, "'cause I don't. Everything was going to be paid for, wasn't it? The car and hotel cost me a fortune. I've got about a hundred dollars left in my wallet. What have you got?"

I did some quick calculations in my head. "Nothing," I said.

"So, what do we do?" Paul asked.

"Mug someone?" I offered. "Recycle some cans? I read somewhere that there's a good soup kitchen down on Ninth Avenue. . . ."

Dad and Paul didn't seem to jump at my ideas.

"Let's just go to Imaginator," I said. "We'll think of something."

They both snorted and shook their heads like I was a meat-head. As the light changed and I followed the crowd across Thirty-fourth Street, I sent out a prayer that these freaks wouldn't make us go home early.

I needed to come up with a solution, fast.

Imaginator

Paul and I bolted the last fifty yards up Thirty-third Street, dodging through the crowd. Dad lumbered along behind.

An Imaginator banner hung from the side of the convention center next to a digital billboard sign. The banner read,

IMAGINATOR FESTIVAL OF INVENTIONS AND CREATIVITY

13–15 MARCH

Today was March 14.

I joined Paul at the end of the short line at a table set out just inside the entrance.

"I can't believe we're actually here."

"Check that out," Paul said, pointing.

A girl was sitting on the ground nearby, back against the wall. She was small with dark hair and eyes. She looked like her parents must've been from someplace interesting.

"Yeah, she's pretty cute," I said.

"No, look what she's doing," Paul said, annoyed.

She was typing into a black glove on her left hand, then she put her hand up to her ear and started talking into it.

"What is that, like, a glove phone?" I asked, as we shuffled forward in line.

"Maybe you can get them here."

"Check out the skates," I said.

On her feet she had these giant wheels. Actually, they were more like bowling balls set into the bottom of a pair of boots. Like one-wheel rollerskates. Rollerballs, maybe.

"How do you balance on those things?" Paul asked. We'd been working on our own style of a two-wheel skateboard for a couple of years and now we were trying to develop a one-wheel board. The balance thing was a killer.

"I could film her on your phone. Why don't you go ask her for a demo?" I said.

Paul just looked at me, rolling his eyes—his "don't be an idiot" look. We both knew by now that Paul wasn't the kind of guy who just went up and talked to humans. Especially girls.

She finished her call.

"I'm gonna go ask her," I said. "Those skates are so good."

"Next!" said a voice.

A round, gray-faced woman peered at us from across the table. Imagine that someone Photoshopped the head of a bulldog onto the body of a rhinoceros and locked it in a ticket booth. That was her.

I took a last look at Rollergirl, hoping she wouldn't take off. "Um, yeah, two tickets, thanks."

The bulldog stared at me. "Really?" she asked. "*You two* want tickets?"

Paul had his usual bed head, and I looked a little rough in my lost-and-found-box threads, but surely we could still go inside?

"Yeah. Two tickets, please," I said.

"Okay. Seven-fifty each for a two-day pass. Show finishes tomorrow," she grunted.

I rustled around in my pocket for the cash Dad had given me. I tossed a ten and a five onto the counter. The woman stared at the notes, then up at me.

"It's seven *hundred* and fifty dollars each," she said.

"Are you kidding?" I said. "We don't want to *buy* the festival."

"Imaginator is not a public exhibition. It's a major industry conference and festival for international delegates. Now, would you like a ticket, sir? If not, please step out of the line."

Paul began moving away, but I held my ground. I didn't want to have to pull this card, but . . .

"We're from Coolhunters," I said. "The website."

She gave me that same bitter, bulldog stare. If she were a real dog, I'd have started backing up real slow.

"Good for you," she said. "Now step aside."

I wanted to chuck her a treat and say, "Chew on this." But I didn't. I moved away.

"Why didn't you know this?" Paul asked.

"Me?"

"Yeah, you. You're the one who lured me here for this," he said.

"As if. What, you don't have access to the web? You couldn't have looked at the site?"

"You were, like, in charge. You kept on talking about it. I figured you might have looked at the prices!" he said.

If we were at home in our workshop I'd have wrestled him to the ground and sat on him, but there was a security dude nearby who looked like he might deport us.

"That ticket chick's pretty special, huh?" said a voice.

It was Rollergirl, standing on her skates now, gently rolling back and forth.

"Yeah," I said. "I mean, not really. Can't you get in either?"

"Nope. I'm Melody," she said.

"Hey. Good to meet you."

"You have a name?"

"Mac. Sorry. And Paul."

Paul's eyes were fixed on her glove. Mine drifted to her skates.

"I heard your accents," she said. "Where are you guys from?"

I liked the way she said "you guys."

"Kings Bay. It's halfway around the world from here," I said.

"Get out. I've heard of Kings Bay. It's, like, the coolest surfing town ever."

"Really?" I said.

"Absolutely."

"Right. That's cool you've heard of it."

I could feel the conversation kind of dying.

"Bummer about the fest," Melody said. "I even tried flirting with the security guy, but he's unbreakable."

"There's gotta be some way in," I said. "We came thousands of miles for this."

"Yeah, well, *bonne chance*," she said, and started rolling away.

"Hey, can I have a look at your glove . . . thing?" Paul said.

He must've really dug the glove to be brave enough to speak to her.

She stopped and turned back.

"Um, sure," she said, not looking so certain.

"What does it do?" Paul asked.

"It's a kind of . . . laptop, I guess. I call it a handtop. And it's a phone and Internet device. It's whatever you want it to be."

"Where did you get it?" I asked.

"I kind of made it myself."

Paul and I looked at her.

"No way," Paul said.

"Yeah way."

"We're inventors too," I said. "Are you gonna sell these or . . ."

She started rolling backward again.

"Not really. Look, I gotta go. Nice to meet you, boys."

She gave us a peace sign and skated off.

"Can you tell me about your skates?" I called.

"I'm late," she said above the noise of traffic and the crowds. People were crisscrossing between us now. But I couldn't let her go. She was a coolhunter's dream.

"Is there someplace we can catch up? Or can we get your number?" I asked, walking toward her as she rolled backward. Then she called out something like "Hog Bender. 17464."

"What?" I yelled.

But she was gone, skating off down Eleventh Avenue. It wasn't like regular skating. She just kept her feet together and leaned forward, and the balls drove her along the sidewalk.

"What the hell is Hog Bender 167646?" I asked Paul.

"Not Hog Bender. Dog Bender. And she said 17464."

"Yeah, well, what's that?" I said, unzipping my bag to grab a pen.

"I dunno. Maybe it's a street," he said.

"Yeah, right. Dog Bender Street. Is that off Cat Twister Ave.?"

I wrote "Dog Bender 17464" on my hand.

"You're not falling in love again, are you?" Paul asked.

"Shut up," I said. He always accused me of falling in love with any girl we met. I think it was because he was hot on them but he didn't have the guts to do anything about it.

"She's gone, anyway. Let's go check messages, see if Speed and Tony have sent us anything."

"Yeah, right," Paul said. "Like we'll ever hear from those idiots again."

← where R u? →

I punched in my password. Paul and Dad were looking over my shoulder, with bated breath. We were at a *massive* Internet café. Like, officially the world's biggest. It looked like central command for a space shuttle launch, hundreds of computers sprawled across a giant room. It was weird seeing my dad in a place like this. He still thought e-mail was cutting-edge technology.

My Coolhunters page came up. Coolhunters was a major social networking site where you registered and shared your cool finds with tens of thousands of other hunters. But there were only six featured hunters on the site, including Paul and me. The six of us were profiled on the home page, and we'd all been invited to New York. There were areas of my Coolhunters world the public could access, and then there was the private side where I talked to friends and did Coolhunters business stuff.

I scanned my messages. A few from Jewels back in Kings

Bay. (I was still trying to work out if she was my girlfriend or not. I'd known her since we were kids, but in the past few weeks, things had been getting a little weird. Good weird. I think.) I had a bunch of messages from African businessmen offering me large amounts of cash if I'd just send them my bank account details. One from Denson, my kitesk8boarding friend. Nothing from Speed or Tony.

"Where'd you say that soup kitchen was?" Dad asked, standing behind me, reading over my shoulder.

"Don't say that," I said.

"It's true. I have no money. We're in all sorts of trouble."

"I'll IM them," I said "And there're phones on the wall over there. You go call them one last time."

I handed Paul my little New York book. "Numbers are on the inside back cover."

"It's not worth it," Paul said.

"Just go."

"Whatever, Mac," he said as he began snaking his way toward the exit.

My dad followed him. "I'll be out front. Don't be long. I've got to take the rental car back," he barked over his shoulder. My dad was a CDS sufferer. Cranky dad syndrome—suffered by fathers everywhere, but my dad's case was chronic.

I quickly punched a subject heading—**where r u?**—and asked Speed to contact us ASAP. Then I logged in to my blog site. I still kept a private blog alongside my Coolhunters one. I started flowing:

new york is so good i want to vomit. we're officially lost. and it's maybe cooler than being found. this city goes blam right in my face. i feel like i'm on the back of something wild and i've got to hold on tight if i don't want to get chucked to the floor. i always half thought new york was a pretend place that i dreamed up. i can't believe somewhere as cool as this actually exists. but it's here. it's real. it's outside my window and in my veins. i want to film everything, only i don't have a camera. and how are you supposed to find cool in a place where everything's cool? how do you decide what's not cool? the fire hydrants and the people and the storefronts and the concrete. the steam coming from gutters. everyone speaking a million different languages all at once. serious looks on their faces and places to go. and the buildings, man. they punch through clouds and make you feel like an ant. it's the maddest place on earth. everywhere else is standing still compared with here. i reckon mexico city or london must feel like ghost towns against new york. i want to see it from above and go down into the sewers and check if there really are alligators down there. i never want to go home. maybe i can stow away here or something, send a postcard to people at home every couple of years, let 'em know how i'm getting on. tell 'em about a new invention i've created or a new book i've put out or a movie i've made. maybe i'll disappear into the crowd by myself right now and become a new yorker.

"You ready?"

It was Paul. So much for disappearing into the crowd.

"Any luck?" I said, but his face told the story: no money. Big city. Ten thousand miles from home. The outlook wasn't hot. I typed **Be scary. Mac** and logged out of my blog. Then I checked my Coolhunters page one last time. You won't believe what landed.

Mac!!!

We just got in. Literally five minutes ago. Flight delayed twelve hrs due 2 storms in Amsterdam. So sorry we missed you @ airport. Paul's phone isn't working!!!! Our phone carrier has messed up our int'l roaming too. I'm sorry. Will make it up to you.

We're at:

The Ludlow Boutique Hotel

Ludlow St

Lower East Side

The hotel is amazing. I'm in room 2503.

Trust you'll get this soon.

Speed

The Ludlow

I slipped the card into the slot, the light flashed green, and I shoved the door open. My jaw hit the floor. Paul pushed past me, into the room.

"Holy ratballs!" he said, running straight for the stairs.

My dad's eyes were like two full moons. We'd never seen anything like this in our lives. Floor-to-ceiling windows with views all over Manhattan and out to the river. A gargantuan living room. A grand piano in one corner to my right, and a kitchen next to it. The furniture was totally wacky. A red pod-shaped seat swinging from the ceiling, right next to an antique couch.

The door leading off to a bathroom was pointy rather than square at the top. It looked like something you'd find in a mosque or something. I ran to the window and looked out. I could see the Chrysler Building up through the sea of high-rises, and the very tip of the Empire State Building.

"Come check this out!" Paul screamed from upstairs. I

leaped up the curving glass staircase to the second floor, which looked down over the living room and out to the city beyond. Paul was jumping up and down on one of two giant beds with posts on the corners and mosquito nets draped over the top. There were iPod docks on the bedside tables. A door led to an adjoining bathroom that was bright orange with glass walls overlooking the city. An egg-shaped tub sat in the middle of the room.

"Geez, this is all right," I heard my dad say from downstairs.

"All right?" I yelled to him. "This is mental! I knew these guys'd pull through."

"Hey, look," Paul said, jumping off the bed, landing awkwardly, and smashing over a pile of boxes in one corner of the room. He didn't even complain. He picked up the envelope that fell off the top and pulled out a card. It read,

Paul,
Enjoy!

There was another pile of boxes next to it with a note for me on top. Paul and I started ripping into the packages. There was a new high-def camera to replace the one we'd lost during our Coolhunters trial back in Kings. There was a new phone each and a whole bunch of clothes—T-shirts, jeans, socks, boxes of new sneaks, even a suit. I ripped off my faded, torn, and patched green cords and pulled on a pair of dark denim jeans. I peeled off my long-sleeve, no-name T that I'd nabbed out of the lost-and-found box back at the arts village, and I grabbed a T-shirt with a picture of a piranha on the front. I checked myself out in the mirror.

I actually looked good. I didn't even look like me. I'd never had a new piece of clothing in my life. Except underwear. And even then, I was pretty sure a few of my pairs were hand-me-downs from my cousins.

"What's all this gear?" Dad asked, arriving at the top of the stairs.

"I don't know," I said.

Paul had already ditched his pile of stuff. He'd opened a pack of games and was choosing FIFA players on the flat-screen TV.

The phone rang, and I somersaulted across the bed.

"I'm takin' a shower," Dad said, and headed back downstairs.

I grabbed the phone.

"Yep!" I said.

"Settling in okay?" Speed said in his London accent. "Look, Mac, I really am sorry about—"

"Forget it!" I said. "Are you kidding me? I *loved* being lost in New York, and I'd stay in that rathole we were in last night for six months if it meant a night in this place. Do we really get to stay here, or is this a joke? 'Cause if it's—"

Speed laughed.

"Yes, mate. You get to stay. Be downstairs in fifteen. There's a restaurant called Mash three doors down the street where we're having lunch. You can meet the other coolhunters there, and I'll be setting the challenge for the week. Don't be late, okay?"

The line went dead.

I slammed the phone down, lay back on the bed, and slapped myself across the face. I was awake. And it hurt a bit.

Mash

"You guys are going to be *massive* stars," said Speed, addressing the group. Under the table, Paul kicked my foot. He had this dream of being famous for something. Kind of weird for a total hermit, but I think he wanted people to admire him from a distance.

Me, Paul, Dad, Speed, Tony, and the other four coolhunters were seated around a big dining table at Mash, a "comfort food" restaurant serving stuff like mashed potatoes and grilled cheese on toast and charging the big bucks for it. Speed called it retro, but it just looked like dinner at Paul's place to me. The walls were bare brick, and Jimi Hendrix was playing on a stereo out back.

"We have *the* most unbelievably incredible plans in place for total world domination. Web, mobile, print, TV, games, virtual worlds, and media that haven't even been invented yet. And *you guys* are going to be the face of it."

My dad snorted under his breath. He'd always taught me

to be wise to people who made big promises. I elbowed him to shut him up. He was the only parent who had showed for lunch, so Paul and I already looked freaky enough without him snorting at our boss.

"Now, before I go on, I want everyone to give due props to our newest hunters on the site, Mac and Paul," said Speed.

Luca, the South American dude who was into adventure sports, gave a couple of lame claps, but when no one else joined in he let it go. I looked at Paul and my dad. The three of us were not like anybody else at the table. Maybe it was our eight-dollar haircuts (I think Paul actually cut his own) or Dad's dirty jeans, checked lumberjack shirt and out-of-control brows. Maybe it was something in our wide-eyed looks that said "backwater hicks." Whatever it was, I knew we didn't belong.

"That was great, guys," said Speed, straight-faced. "A really warm welcome."

Michiko, the Japanese photographer chick from Paris, was playing with her bangs, not even listening. Her skateboard was on the table, lying between her knife and fork. Next to Michiko was Van (short for Vanessa), who described herself on the site as a tech expert and New York City rich kid. She had one earbud in and was staring right through us. I smiled but got nothing. Then there was Rash, the music and movie buff from Shanghai, China. His profile said he was scared of going outside. He sat there, hoodie on, slumped down, eyes lit by a handheld games machine he was playing. Luca was the only one so far who'd lowered himself to speak to us.

Speed and Tony, the site's founders, were at the head of the table. Speed had big sunglasses shading his eyes and a black v-neck T-shirt with PRADA on it. Tony, who wore a suit, was older. I hadn't heard him speak much, but he had power. It felt like he was the money guy.

"Anyway," Speed said. "Here are the rules of the game. We need you guys to find *the* coolest stuff in the city. Vlog it, blog it, photograph it, draw it, paint it, Etch A Sketch it. Whatever. So long as you're uncovering stuff that *nobody* knows is here and that everyone wants a piece of. We want the Next Big Thing. You need to upload a fresh find to the site every day and keep on delivering, keep the punters coming back for more. Any day you don't deliver something, you're gone. You'll be paid a hundred and fifty a day for the five days you're here and, as always, we'll cover hotel and expenses."

Paul and I gave each other five under the table. It'd take us, like, two million years to earn seven hundred and fifty bucks each in our old McJobs at Taste Sensation, a skanky burger joint on the main street of Kings.

Speed went on. "Coolhunting is not a job you keep forever. You stay as long as the site subscribers like you, as long as they're logging on to your part of the site and looking to you for fresh stuff. Think of it as sudden death every day. I'd like all of you to be there on our next international hunt, in Shanghai, Rash's hometown, in three months' time, but at least one of you won't be. We are getting in excess of a million hits a day, and all of those people want your job. One of you is going home this week."

Van straightened in her chair. Michiko looked like she was about to spit at Speed.

"I don't mind if you enjoy yourselves, but we are deadly serious about the business of cool," Speed went on. "There are copycat sites cropping up all over the web, and we need to know about trends happening on the street before the innovators even think of them. Got it?"

Everybody nodded.

"Good. This is your chance to prove yourselves. Go hard or go home," Speed said, staring directly at me and Paul. "Dig in."

As the others started eating, I looked around the table. I was pretty sure that I must've read and dreamed more about this city than any of these dudes, even Van, who lived here.

"He's a bit of a goose," Dad said in a low voice. I elbowed him.

"They all think we're losers," Paul whispered out of the side of his mouth.

"I don't care," I said.

I actually did care, but there was no point in talking about it. I'd already decided I was going to blow them out of the water with the stuff we found, no matter what it took to find it. By the end of the week we were gonna own New York. I was sure of it.

← The Hunt →

A kid pulled a killer airwalk, grabbing the nose of his board and kicking his feet out, then chucking the board back beneath him before landing and caning down the half-pipe. And this thing was huge, the biggest pipe I'd ever laid eyes on.

"That's, like, three stories high!" Paul said, almost not believing what he was seeing.

Paul, Dad, and I were gawking at the skaters through a rusty wire fence. The pipe was in the back of an empty block that had a burned-out car in the middle of it. It was hemmed in by tall buildings on three sides, graffiti everywhere.

Another kid dropped in and went tearing down the face to shoot up the other side, pulling a big old handplant, fingers on the lip, board in the air, before pushing off and firing back down again.

"Let's shoot it," I said, lifting the wire and sliding under the fence.

It was 10:15 a.m. Friday, our first proper day of coolhunting, and I figured if we were going to find the real New York and prove we weren't bumpkin freaks from the wrong side of the planet, we were going to have to push the boundaries a little. We were in the Lower East Side, a few blocks from the hotel. The area felt kind of sketchy, but then it had clubs and expensive restaurants and stores sprinkled around too. We'd been hunting for this doughnut shop I had a picture of in my New York book, but doughnuts would have to wait.

"Don't be ridiculous," my dad said.

"These dudes will smoke us," Paul said.

"They look young," I said. "We'll be fine."

"Have you not seen an American movie before?" Paul asked. "We're not in Kings Bay. Just shoot it from back here."

"We'll hardly even get a picture. And we'll have to zoom in so much it'll be all shaky."

"This is so typical of you, Mac. You'd rather get a steady picture than keep your life," Paul said.

"I'm going in," I said, and headed off across the block, pulling the HD cam out of my backpack. It was a beautiful machine. I'd spent all night figuring it out.

Dad groaned and said, "Wait a minute," awkwardly scrambling under the wire. Paul stood there for a second, but there was no way he was staying out there by himself, so he slipped under, too. We headed across the block toward the skaters.

There were three or four guys riding the pipe and another six or seven hanging out, pulling moves on rails and other junk lying around. They all looked our age or younger. Kids as young as eight or nine, even. They had guts to ride that ramp. There was no way I'd have done it when I was nine. Or maybe even now.

One of them had a plaster cast on his arm. It was painted red and covered in graffiti tags. Another kid was skating with his ankle bandaged. A guy and a girl were playing b-ball using a milk crate as a hoop.

"I think we should stop here," Paul said when we were halfway down the block.

"I agree," Dad said, which was his way of saying, "I'm freaking out, but I want you to make your own decision." That was my folks' one rule on parenting: Let him make his own decisions. It had gotten me into some pretty bad situations, but at least I got to find out what happened when I did dumb stuff, rather than having someone always tell me I shouldn't.

I talked them into moving a little closer, and we scooched down behind the burned-out car, where we couldn't be seen. There was a blackened BMW badge lying in the dirt. I set up the camera, dragging a three-legged chair over to use as a tripod. I pushed the chair out past the rear bumper so I could stay hidden and still shoot the action.

"Shouldn't we ask them first?" Paul said, on his knees behind the car. "Get them to sign a release?"

"Then they'll play to the camera," I said. "I want to shoot the real deal. We'll ask them later. They'll love it."

I started filming. One tiny kid was getting ready to roll. I zoomed right in on his face. It was a bit pixelly, but you could see him staring into the pipe, psyching himself up. A couple of the others were going, "Whoo. Whoo. Whoo," trying to fire him up. Then, all of a sudden, he let go. I crash-zoomed out. His board dropped away from him and he free-fell three storys, landing on his back on the curve of the ramp and rolling into the center of the half-pipe.

He lay there, still, for a few seconds, and a couple of the others ran in to see him, crowding around. Slowly he pulled himself up and, as he did, three other dudes dropped off the lip. One of them stacked, but two pulled off some crazy moves: airwalks, nollie big spins, and kickflips.

"This is so good," I said to Paul.

He could see the action on the flip screen.

"Sincerely," he said.

I pushed the chair out from the car a little farther to get a bit more of the half-pipe in the shot. The chair scraped loudly across the concrete, and I heard a "Hey, what're you doin'?"

I ducked back in behind the car so I was fully hidden.

"Hey, yo," said the voice again.

"What do we do?" I asked Paul.

"Don't ask me!" he said.

So I stood up slowly, ready to explain.

"Hey," I said.

They didn't look that happy to see me.

"You guys want to be on the web?" I asked.

"What?" said the guy closest to us. He had a black cap on backward, bandanna underneath, black armbands, T-shirt with Japanese script, two belts, a moon tan, zits on his chin.

"Coolhunters. This site. I'm shooting some . . ."

Four or five of them started walking toward us. One of them picked up a bit of wood, another grabbed what looked like a metal pole.

My mouth ran dry. "They're coming," I said to Dad and Paul, who were still behind the car.

Seconds later our feet were pounding across the deserted block, jumping scrubby bushes, landing on bits of mashed-up tar. I could hear the guys screaming behind us, giving chase. Then I fell, grazing my hands pretty bad and scratching the camera. The voices were closing in behind. I dragged myself up, bolted toward the wire, then skidded beneath it. I held the fence up for Paul as he slid under, and I looked back to see where Dad was, but he still had maybe twenty yards to go. The kids were almost on top of him, and he was no athlete.

"C'mon, Dad! Go!" I screamed.

I could either go back in for him or just stand there and shout for him to run faster.

Escape

"Don't, man," Paul said as I slipped under the wire and back into the empty block. But what was I going to do? Leave my old man for dead? I made it to the other side as the front kid came within striking distance of my dad, who still had maybe ten yards to run.

"Hey! Stop! Stop!" I screamed, running toward them and looking around for something to defend myself with, even though I wouldn't really know how. All that peace and love stuff growing up hadn't prepared me for a situation like this. Kings Bay wasn't exactly the 'hood.

So I stuck my hands in the air, trying to show that we weren't there to start something. Dad made it to me, out of breath. He turned and we came face-to-face with them. They were wearing a mix of baseball, basketball, and skate gear. One kid wore a black T-shirt with I SKATE NY on it, but instead of the word *skate* it had a picture of a board. He wore a beanie over messy blond hair. He was younger than me and kind of skinny looking, but he had an ugly piece of wood in his hand with a few nails sticking out of it.

"Gimme the camera," he said.

I felt the cam sitting there in my sweaty palm. I didn't move.

"I said, gimme the camera."

"Give him the camera," Paul said, and when I resisted, my dad grabbed it out of my hand and walked over, giving it to the dude. I don't want to tell you exactly what they said next, but they kind of asked us to leave.

Dad and I backed toward the fence. He pull the wire up, and I crawled through to the other side. When Dad was under, the three of us crossed the street and started heading back up the block. They watched us go, trying to look tough, which I guess they were. Beanie dude showed the other guys the camera, turning it over in his hands and laughing. One of them shouted something at us as they headed back across the block toward the ramp.

Dad, Paul, and I kept walking. Dad was out of breath, and my heart was thumping somewhere up inside my head. Paul was muttering stuff to himself, trying to process what had happened. We didn't say anything for ages, until we came to a park and all collapsed on a bench.

"Sorry," I said.

Dad and Paul didn't say anything. Which was good in a way. They could have screamed at me and told me I'd nearly killed them.

"You nearly killed us," Paul said.

"It was a stupid idea, goin' in there," my dad said.

"I know," I said. "And then we gave them our freaking camera!"

"Forget the camera," Dad said. "That was the smartest thing we did."

"You're banned from making decisions from now on," Paul said.

"Hear, hear," Dad agreed.

I knew I'd been wrong, so I tried to bite my tongue and not snap at Paul.

"That half-pipe was brutal," I said. "I'd love to have a go."

They both looked at me with filthy disdain.

Dad got up. Paul followed. Then I went too. We walked up Grand Street, right past my doughnut shop.

"Hey, Doughnut Plant," I said, busting out my New York book and flipping to the page. "Says here they sell square doughnuts the size of my head. Who wants one?"

They turned to see.

"We haven't had a doughnut all day," I said. "We could die or something."

We bought three and sat out front and ate them. I had blackberry jelly, and it was definitely the best thing I've ever tasted in my life. I filmed Paul eating his on my new phone, which only made me feel worse about giving up the camera. Then we sat there and watched girls walk by wearing boots and short skirts with scraggly bits of material hanging off them. One chick was wearing angel wings. A dude went by in a shirt that looked like it was made out of Paul's mom's curtains. Everyone seemed to wear thick black glasses like Paul's too. I filmed it all.

"Who knew there was a place on earth where your glasses were cool?" I said to Paul. He got me in a headlock and knuckled me. The sugar hit had lifted the mood a little.

"Where do you pair want to drag me to now?" Dad grunted, his face still red, his breathing wheezy.

"Get another doughnut?" I said.

"Go home," said Paul, releasing me. "To Kings."

"Why?" I asked him.

"Because ever since we left there our lives have been a disaster. Bad flight. Abandoned at the airport. Bags lost. Then the car crash."

"We didn't crash," I said.

"Nearly," Paul snapped back. "Then I had to shower in blood—"

"Rust," I said.

"Whatever," he said. "We couldn't get into Imaginator, which is the one thing I came to New York to do. These other coolhunter idiots are total arrogant snobs. And I don't know if you noticed, but we were almost killed by a bunch of preschoolers and their wooden blocks about twenty minutes ago. This place is bumming me out."

When he put it like that, I could kind of see how he might not have had the greatest two days of his life.

"But what about all the doughnuts?" I said, raising my brows. "And the sausages and egg whites you had at that Mash joint."

He didn't even look at me.

I pulled my New York book out.

"Put it away," Paul said.

"What?"

"There's nothing cool in there."

"What do you mean?"

"You cut those pictures out of tourist brochures, man. These guys want cutting-edge cool. Coolhunters is not for retirees on vacation."

I flicked the book open, determined to prove him wrong, and came to rest on a page with a girl skating down by the East River.

"What about Melody—the girl with the handtop glove and the crazy skates?" I said to him.

Paul groaned and shook his head, but I could tell he liked the angle.

"What if we try to find her again?" I said.

"And what? Coolhunt her? With no video camera? What are we gonna do, paint a picture of her and write a poem about it? That sucks."

Paul's new phone rang. "Crazy Frog" style. It was his mom.

He wandered away to talk to her. I listened to see if he told her all the bad stuff that had happened. He didn't, thank God. She'd have been on the next plane over, and that would have been worse than getting mugged by a gang of toddlers. Mrs. Porter hung on way too tight. She was, like, the opposite of my mom. If Paul didn't have me, he'd never get into any trouble. He'd be a shell of a man.

When he got off the phone, I checked the map in my book and we headed for the hotel. From there, Dad called the airline. His and Paul's bags had spent two days in Taipei, but they'd finally arrived in New York City and the airline had them delivered to us. Paul refused to leave the room for the rest of the day. He sat and watched reruns of *Saved by the Bell* and a *SpongeBob SquarePants* marathon. Dad slept for hours. I put the Doughnut Plant piece up on Coolhunters, then prowled around the room like a caged beast, trying to work out how I'd break it to Speed that I'd given a five-thousand-dollar HD camera to a bunch of really scary nine-year-olds on a vacant block somewhere in the Lower East Side.

Surely he'd understand.

Dog Bender

The doughnut piece was weak. Subscribers hate it.

You have to deliver better than this.

Look at what the others uploaded.

Speed

I logged out of my Coolhunters messages and googled **dog bender 17464** on my phone. A message popped up: **No results found for "dog bender 17464."**

I was down in the lounge area of our hotel room. It was 5:00 a.m., and I'd been up for two hours already. The jet lag was killing me. I paced around on the thick, red shag rug. It felt good between my toes. My dad was sleeping on the floor under the stairs on a thick rolled-up blanket he'd brought from home. The sky was starting to grow orange over Manhattan.

I punched in **hog bender 17464**. I'd never actually owned a cell phone before (one of the downsides of having lo-fi, enviro-warrior parents), so I was pretty slow and useless with my thumbs. Then I tried **dogbender street new york** and about seven hundred other combos, but I got nothing.

After yesterday's disaster, and now with Speed on my case, I figured I had to work fast if I was going to turn this trip around. The rollerballs and computer glove that girl Melody was wearing were the most coolhuntable thing we'd discovered, apart from the three-story half-pipe. If I could just work out the cryptic clue the rollerball chick had left, we'd at least get an interview and have something decent to put on the site.

But it was useless. For all I knew, she might have said "Bog Blender" or "Hot Dog Vendor" or "My middle name is Glenda" (although she didn't really seem like a Glenda). Trying to find one girl in a city of nearly nine million people was loco.

I grabbed my New York book off the coffee table and flopped onto the couch. What was Paul saying, "retirees on vacation"? I flipped through. The bottom corner of every page was grubby from me thumbing it so often in the lead-up to the trip. There was a pic of the Statue of Liberty and a note I'd jotted saying, "Free tickets 2 see statue on Staten Island ferry." There was a picture of Economy Candy (a cool candy shop downtown) and one of the Empire State Building. There was a shot of a hidden tunnel under Chinatown and an image of FAO Schwarz, a massive toy store. I turned the page, and there was a snap from the Imaginator site opposite a clipping about the world's biggest secondhand bookstore. There was a pic of a New York Police Department cap. I chucked the book onto the coffee table. Paul was right. None of this stuff was break-ing news.

I logged back in to Coolhunters and re-read the message from Speed, then I checked out what Van, Michiko, Luca, and Rash had put up. Van had discovered an unknown indie band's latest release, available only on ancient audiocassette. No download. So you had to track down a tape player just to lis-ten to their album. . . . Freaks. Rash had interviewed an inde-pendent game creator. Michiko was a fan of hot sauces, and she reckoned she'd found the hottest in the world somewhere in Tribeca. Luca had covered a company doing rappelling off skyscrapers. (This, I had to admit, was cool.)

Speed's message had come in at 4:33 a.m., half an hour earlier. I figured he must've been jet-lagged, too. I hadn't broken the news about the camera. He was still online, so I sat there trying to work out what to say to him. Eventually, I pinged him a message.

Hey S. I got 2 tell u something. If not sitting down maybe u should. We haven't got a cam. M.

I waited. Then, a few seconds later:

Speed: What?! You lost another 1?

The camera Speed had given us for our trial back in Kings Bay had been stolen from our workshop.

Mac: Yeah. Yesterday. We kind of got mugged.

Speed: And they took the camera?

Mac: We gave it 2 them. So they wouldnt kill us.

Speed: So its gone?

Mac: Yep.

Speed didn't respond. I sat there, quietly stressing. After a couple of minutes, I couldn't take it anymore.

Mac: Really sry Speed.

No response.

Mac: Do u think there might be another cam 4 us to use?

Speed: No. Sort yrself out or you're gone.

Speed went offline.

I hit the elevator button and the door sprang open. Van was inside.

"Hey," I said, feeling pretty miserable.

She raised her brows at me, the minimum she could do to acknowledge I was alive.

I pressed the button to close the doors, and we began moving. It was a glass elevator, and you could see twenty-four floors down into the lobby, where the guests looked like mice. My stomach flipped as we fell.

"You staying here?" I asked her.

She did the brow-raise again.

"I thought, maybe, with you being a New Yorker you might not be."

No reaction. Not even a look. The elevator stopped on the fourteenth floor. By then I was starting to despise her. A guy stepped in, the doors closed, and we started moving again.

"Hey, did I tell you I know someone just like you in the town where I live?"

Van did a slow look toward me.

"Tell me you don't mean Cat," she said.

Cat DeVrees had competed against me back in Kings Bay for the coolhunting job. She was a spoiled but incredibly hot chick with anger running through her veins. I'd forgotten the other hunters would have seen her vlogs on the site.

"Um," I said.

"She was a total cow in that trial," Van said. "You don't even know me."

"You've snubbed me twice," I said.

"What are you talking about? Have you even tried to talk to me till now?"

I thought about it for a second. I hadn't.

"Don't pin your insecurities on me," she said, and started typing a message into her phone.

The door opened. She stepped out into the lobby, still texting. I followed.

"Hey, you're a local. Can you tell me something?" I said, catching up to her.

"Yeah, it's not like I'm busy or anything. What?"

"I met this girl. . . ."

"Congratulations."

"No, that's not it," I said. "I met this girl and I asked how I could get in touch with her, and she said to me, 'Hog bender' or 'Dog bender 17464.' What does that mean?"

"Dog bender?" She started laughing.

"Something like that."

"Try 'Dawg Finder,'" she said, going back to her phone.

"What's that?"

"Have you got GPS on your cell?"

"My what?"

"Your phone," she said, like she was explaining something to a two-year-old.

"I don't know," I said. "It's the same as yours, so . . ."

"It's an app that lets you find your friends—your dawgs—on a map. The number would've been her finder code. Look. . . ."

Van stopped at the entrance to the hotel restaurant and showed me her phone. There was a map of Manhattan with four or five little red dots flashing. She hit a button and zoomed in on one of the dots, and you could see the street names.

"My friend Roxy is only half a block from here, so I could go see her right now if I wanted," Van said. "If you want to go undercover you hit 'phantom' and they can't see you anymore."

"That's cool," I said. "Thanks. And sorry about the Cat thing."

"Forget about it," she said. "You remind me of my brother. And he's a total loser."

A guy showed us to our seats. He thought we were together, but Van sat two tables away.

I found Dawg Finder, joined, and punched in Melody's code. Then I messaged her and asked her to be my dawg. I called out to Van and asked if she wanted to be my dawg too. She said, "No way."

"Thanks," I said. "Appreciate it."

I headed for the buffet. I hadn't eaten cooked food at home in a year. My ma reckoned cooking disturbed the spiritual essence of the food or something, but I'd had just about all the raw cabbage and zucchini I could hack. I piled plate after plate with bacon, eggs, mushrooms, hash browns, pastries, muffins, omelette, and toast.

Around plate number six, Dad and Paul arrived. By plate nine I could feel this freaky food concoction swilling around in my belly. That's when Melody messaged me and her icon flipped up on my Dawg Finder map.

Paul and I got ready to roll.

"You boys have fun," Dad said, his face hidden behind the *New York Times*.

"You're not coming?" I asked, my stomach groaning under the weight of nine full breakfasts.

"Nah, you'll be all right."

Paul and I looked at each other. After yesterday, was he kidding?

"Are there any rules or anything?" Paul whispered to me.

"Are there any rules?" I asked Dad.

He folded his paper down, a little annoyed at being disturbed. "I don't know. Do you want rules?"

Paul and I thought about it. I hadn't lived with my dad in years. He wasn't used to making stuff up to pretend he was in control. I shrugged.

"Just don't stray too far from the hotel," he said, satisfied he'd fulfilled his parental responsibilities. "You'll be all right. Go and have fun. I'm taking the detector up to Central Park."

Dad had brought his metal detector from home. On a Sunday afternoon in Kings, he could find a few hundred in cash and jewelry on the beach. Kids at school gave me a hard time about it, said he was a scavenger. I looked at Van, hoping she hadn't heard him.

Dad flipped his paper up in front of his face again, and that was that.

Paul and I hit the street. We were on a mission to find Melody, get Speed back on our side, and keep our coolhunting careers alive.

⊲ Alphabet City ⊳

Paul and I whipped around a corner off Houston Street and hurried down an alley. We were in a part of town known as Alphabet City. It was Saturday morning, and people were everywhere. Sitting around, drinking coffee, eating bagels, talking loudly. The thin street was lined with dozens of cafés and small clothes stores. (The stores were small. Not the clothes.) Fire escapes jutted out from buildings above us.

I looked at the icon flashing on my phone.

"She's just here somewhere," I said to Paul.

There was a line of about thirty people winding out of a store up ahead. Paul and I cruised past the people, scanning for Melody. I had only a hazy memory of what she looked like. Short, cute, and Italian looking.

We came to the shopfront, but no Melody. Howls of laughter echoed out into the alley. A crackly painted sign above the tiny hole-in-the-wall shop read TICKLE SHOP—TICKLING NEW YORKERS SINCE 1983. Paul and I pressed our faces up against the dirty glass. Inside there were two seats, like dentist's chairs, and two Asian women tickling people. One customer, who looked about twenty, was having her arms tickled with a long pink feather and giggling uncontrollably. The kid next to her was only about our age, and the woman was really digging him in the ribs with her fingers. He was screaming with laughter. I started laughing just watching it.

A sheet of paper was stuck to the window with crusty, yellow adhesive tape. The word MENU was handwritten at the top, then it listed the different tickle sessions you could choose. There was the Afternoon Breeze, the Japanese Fighting Fish, and the Howler. I figured the ribsy guy must be getting that. It was seven bucks for ten minutes.

A man at the front of the line was wearing a New York Fire Department shirt.

"Popular place," I said. "Always this busy?"

"Are you kidding me? This is quiet," he said.

"Next!" screamed a voice from inside as pink-feather girl went by, wiping tears from her eyes. Fire guy went inside.

"It's weird and dirty," Paul said.

"What's dirty?" I asked him.

"People going in there with warts and scabies and stuff and getting tickled."

"Do you even know what scabies is?" I asked.

He looked at me. "No. But it's bad. And those ticklers are so old. And look how small that filthy little room is."

I peered back in at the tickle room. Suddenly what had seemed pretty innocent—and maybe even fun—was stained with Paul's fear of all things involving dirt, confined spaces, and old people.

"I bet they eat porridge and casseroles," Paul said, looking at the tickling women.

Paul saw this direct connection between old people and sloppy food. He reckoned anyone over thirty must eat casseroles, and he couldn't deal with it.

"I'm shooting it," I said.

"Are you kidding?" Paul asked. "This is not cool. This is scabs. It's worse than the doughnut shop."

I switched my phone to camera. Last night I'd worked out that, once you'd crunched and compressed it for the web, the vid quality on the phone was nearly as good as the HD camera anyway.

"What about Melody?" he asked, desperate to divert me.

"Just gimme a second."

I shot the ticklees and the ticklers, the line down the alley, and the store sign. Then I got Paul to film a quick piece with me talking.

"Hey, I'm Mac Slater. This is the Tickle Shop, established 1983, Alphabet City, New York, New York. I don't care if this is a city secret or if it's way-old news—I reckon this place is cool, and don't be surprised if Tickle Shops start cropping up all over the planet. Remember where you heard it first."

"That's ridiculous," Paul said, hitting the stop button. "It's sick, man. In a bad way. We're fighting for our coolhunting lives here, and you want to deliver this? Tickle shops are so not the future."

Like you'd know, I thought. "Let's find Melody," I said, checking my phone. Her icon was flashing now over on Avenue B, a couple of blocks away. She was on the move. Paul and I broke into a jog.

Avenue B

We dodged up Avenue A and across East Fifth Street. Paul told me I had the phone map upside down, so we went back across East Fifth, then suddenly we were lost. We argued for ten minutes, then asked this dude where Avenue B was.

"You're standin' on it," he said, shaking his head. You know your sense of direction is pretty bad when GPS can't help.

I looked back at the phone, turned around, looked up the street, and saw a girl crouched next to a brown brick building opposite a park called Tompkins Square. She had a backpack on, and a set of paints lay next to her on the ground. Paul and I cruised up the path.

"You sure that's her?" Paul whispered.

She was painting on the wall—a Native American dude wearing a headdress, riding a bull.

"Melody?" I said.

She whipped around, taking a sharp breath. "God, you scared me," she said.

"Sorry. Did you think we were cops?" I asked, kind of hoping she'd say yes. No one had ever mistaken me for a cop before.

"No," she said. "I thought you were some creepy guy."

Not quite what I was looking for.

". . . but you're the guys from the Imaginator, right? Mac and—"

"Paul," I said.

"Right."

"What do you think?" she asked us.

"Nice," I said, looking at the work. It was pretty good.

"It's the Wall Street bull," she said, standing up. "There's a huge statue of a bull down in the Financial District. It stands for, like, economic aggression or something. And this guy here's a Lenape Indian. I liked the idea of him taming Wall Street's butt."

I laughed.

"Aren't you worried about cops?" Paul asked.

"You kidding me?" she asked. "Lock up the artists? This is my gift to the city of New York. Have you guys seen Banksy's or Swoon's stuff?"

"No," I said, shrugging.

"Street art's the lifeblood of the city."

A guy on the other side of the street started screaming at no one in particular. Melody wiped paint off her hands on a cloth and slipped her phone glove on.

I wanted to ask if we could shoot her artwork, but it felt a bit weird so soon after we'd met again.

"I didn't expect you guys to search me out this morning," she said, making me feel like a loser. Then she said, "Wasabi gum?" as she offered a small packet of green pellets. I took one, ate it, chewed. Not bad. I smiled. Then I breathed out. The gum was burning a hole into the center of my brain. My nostrils were on fire. I coughed and squeezed my nose hard.

She grinned. "Good, huh?"

"Great," I choked out, crying but trying to look like everything was cool. "We just don't know that many people, so we thought we'd kind of look you up."

"I'm about to go get a bite," she said. "You wanna roll with? I know the best place. It's across town, but it's worth it."

"Yeah, sure," I said, spitting the gum out into a napkin and pocketing it as soon as she looked away.

She headed off, and Paul raised his palms to me, annoyed. "We should've shot her artwork."

"What? We meet her, and two seconds later we want to bleed her for her coolness? Relax, duders," I said.

We headed off down Seventh Street and over Third Avenue. I loved the street names: They were so New York. Melody ate the town up. It was hard to stay with her as she ducked and weaved in and out of traffic.

I was in desperate need of a drink, so we stopped along the way for bubble tea from a street vendor. Melody couldn't believe we'd never had one before. She ordered two, both lychee flavor, and paid for them. Paul refused to try it.

"Take a sip," she said, sipping on her own. I was a little suspicious after wasabi gum, but I sucked on the big paper straw. Nothing happened. I tried again. Nothing. I jiggled the straw, trying one last time, and a rush of lumps sped up through the straw and down my throat. I nearly barfed them back up again, and she laughed till green stuff came out of her nose.

"It's tapioca," she said, once she got hold of herself. "The lumps."

"This is wrong," I said, and Melody laughed again.

"Stay with it," she said. "I'm hooked."

We started walking again. My near-death-by-tapioca had broken the ice, and we chatted easily after that. Melody thought it was pretty cool that my mom was a fire twirler. I was trying to twist conversation toward her inventions, but she always managed to answer a question with a question. So I told her about the stuff Paul and I had created over the years and our failed attempts to fly.

"That is *so* cool," she said.

Paul hung back a bit, looking miserable (his favorite way to be) and not saying much. His mom called just as we stopped at Broadway. Traffic streamed by, and I saw more cars in three minutes than I'd see in a year in Kings. I was reminded what a hick from Hicksville I was and how much I wanted to live in New York.

"You guys need flying transport here," I said.

"Tell me about it. But where do you take off?" Melody asked.

"Parachute's too messy," I said. "You can't have a million wings filling the sky."

"I have friends who're working on an environmentally friendly jet pack," she said as dozens of yellow cabs tore past.

"Really?"

"Mmmm, but it's got issues," she said. "I think the future's in the personal helicopter. Have you heard about the guy who's come up with foldable rotors so that you can drive around after you land?"

"No," I said. "But Paul and I once made a backpack solo helicopter with ceiling-fan blades."

"Really? Did it work?"

I stopped and rolled up the leg of my jeans to show her the scar.

"Ewww," she said, screwing up her face. "Work in progress, huh?"

I loved showing people my scars.

"There's also that flying car," I said, rolling my jeans back down and catching up to her, "that you can drive on a regular road and then fold out the wings for take-off at an airport?"

"I want one," she said.

"Me too."

There was this weird smile between us for a second.

Something that said, "Hey, you're cool." Well, that's what mine said. Hers might've said, "You have something large sticking out of your left nostril." I wiped just in case, but I didn't feel anything there. By then the moment had passed.

"Have you guys thought about sustainable fuels?" Melody asked.

"We're all over sustainable," I said. "We want to make our own biofuel."

"Do it, baby," she said.

We crossed the street and then cut through Washington Square Park, which I'd read a bunch about. It used to be a cemetery, and they reckon that maybe twenty thousand people are buried beneath the park. I felt bad for walking on their heads. Pretty soon we arrived at a diner in Greenwich Village. Melody shoved the door open and went inside. Paul grabbed my arm.

"Don't tell me we're eating here," he said.

"What do you mean? What's wrong with here?"

Peanut Butter Sandwiches

We were standing outside Peanut Butter & Co., an old-school American sandwich shop.

"I have a nut allergy," Paul said.

"What?"

"If I walk inside that place, I'll probably fall over and die. On the spot."

"You don't have a *nut* allergy," I told him.

"Oh, right, so you're me, are you? You know, do you?"

"I've been your best friend since we were, like, six. So I think I have a pretty good idea of when you're lying like a dog," I said.

"Have you ever seen me eat nuts?"

I tried to think, and I couldn't exactly remember. But what did that mean? What kid carries a pocketful of cashews to snack on? He was lying.

"Not exactly," I said.

"There you go."

"But if you did have a nut allergy, don't you think you

might have mentioned it? Don't nut people have to be, like, on freak-alert for nuts in everything they eat?"

"Do you see me eating a varied diet that might expose me to nuts?"

Maybe that was why he ate so many sausages and egg whites, I thought. But then I remembered. "I've seen you eat chocolate with nuts in it plenty of times," I said accusingly.

"They're . . . not real nuts," he said. "They're—"

"Shut up," I said. "Come inside. Smooth or crunchy?"

"I am allergic to *nuts!*"

"You're allergic to life!" I said. "You make this stuff up just so you don't have to talk to people or do anything. Come inside, sit down. She won't bite."

"I'm outta here," he said, turning and walking off up the street.

"What?" I said. Melody saw me through the glass door and made a face and hand gesture that said, *What's going on?* I motioned to say, *Back in a minute,* however you do that. Then I chased Paul up the street.

"What?" I said again, spinning him around by his shoulder.

"I'm going home."

"Over a peanut butter sandwich?" I said. "This girl is, like, a festival of cool and you're just gonna walk away?"

"You're falling in love again, Mac. Like you did with Cat. Like you do with every girl who doesn't look like a dog's butt. I'm telling Jewels."

"Yeah, good response. I'm in love. That's it. You got me. Are you jealous because I actually opened my mouth and spoke to her?" I said, chasing him across the street and into the park.

Rollerbladers sped by, women breastfed babies, punk dudes sat there looking sick and white, tourists snapped photos in front of the fountain.

I walked around in front of Paul and stopped him.

"You're always saying, 'Be scary,' but what do you do to be scary?" I asked him. "Nothing! You make up all these diseases for yourself. You're all 'Ooooh, help me, Mac. I'm scared of old people, small spaces, flying—and now peanuts!'"

Paul looked at me for a second like he was going to smack me. Then he just pushed right past and continued walking through the park. I let him go. Almost.

"You don't even know where you're going," I yelled. But he kept walking. "Idiot!" I screamed, and everybody looked at me.

"Smooth or crunchy?"

"Crunchy," Melody and I said at the same time.

We were at the counter of Peanut Butter & Co.

"Cinnamon raisin, dark chocolate, white chocolate, honey, maple syrup, spicy, or plain?" she asked.

"Um, spicy?" I said, not really sure.

"Definitely maple," Melody said.

"And would you like Marshmallow Fluff? Strawberry, raspberry, or original?"

I looked at the row of Marshmallow Fluff jars on the counter.

"We'll both have raspberry," Melody said, looking at me. "Trust me. You want raspberry."

We paid and she led us, with our sandwiches, back to a booth. I took a bite.

"Holy . . . ," I said, through a mouthful of peanut butter and Fluff.

"Is that the best thing you've ever tasted, or what?" she asked.

"Better," I said, taking another bite. "This is, like . . ." I couldn't even put into words how good that peanut butter sandwich was. Maybe it was the baked bread. My mom had us on uncooked bread as part of the raw food thing, and that stuff should be banned.

We sat and ate and talked for a while. We talked about Buddhism, which my mom was into and I knew a bit about. Then we talked about art (her mom was an artist), and then we got onto planet hunting.

"Scientists have found more than two hundred planets circling other stars," she told me. "I one hundred percent know that there is other life out there. Did you see they found water on Mars?"

We talked about nuclear weapons for a while (my dad had taught me tons about nuclear power) and then inventing again. She mentioned a place called the Hive, where she creates her stuff. It was the wildest conversation. She seemed to know everything about everything. And I knew a little about some things.

When there was a lull, I pulled out my phone and filmed a bit of the store.

"Nice phone," she said.

"Thanks."

"Where'd you get that?" she asked.

"Um, someone gave it to me," I said.

"Sweet."

My shot came to rest on her.

"I'm kind of a coolhunter," I said, looking at her on the phone screen.

"What?" she said, covering her sandwich-filled mouth with a hand.

"A coolhunter," I said, putting the phone down. It felt weird saying it to her. I don't know why. Maybe because I saw myself more as someone who creates stuff than someone who just reports on things that other people have created. "I find stuff and put it on a website, cool things other people might not see. Hey," I said, trying to make it sound like I'd just thought of it, "do you think you might be able to show me some stuff you've designed sometime? Like, maybe, your glove and your skates, and maybe I could put them on the site?"

"I can't," she said.

"Why not?"

"I just can't really talk about the things I make."

"You're a great speaker. You'll be fine," I said, hitting record.

"That's not what I mean," she said. "I gotta go."

She stood, rocking out of my shot.

"Why?" I asked.

"I have to meet some people."

"Look, if you don't want to show me the skates, just—"

She squeezed out of the booth.

"It's been really nice talking to you. Maybe send me a text before you leave, huh? Catch you round."

I called out, "Okay." Then she headed out the door and onto the street. I watched her go, wondering what I'd said wrong. Why wouldn't she want her stuff on Coolhunters? When she was out of sight, I grabbed my wallet and phone. I figured I'd give Paul a call, see where he was at. But, as I stood up, I saw Melody's phone glove sitting on the seat.

The A Train to Inweird

I rammed the restaurant door open and bolted off in the direction I'd seen Melody go. I scanned streets packed with tourists, street performers, and brunchers. A squirrel scurried up a tree to get out of my way. A couple of BMX kids nearly cleaned me up at an intersection. Then I caught a glimpse of Melody about fifty yards away heading into Washington Square Park, right near where Paul had disappeared.

"Melody!" I screamed, and everyone in the street except her looked around. By the time I got to the park, I couldn't see her anymore. I looked at my phone, hoping to Dawg Find her, but the Melody icon was winking at me on the very spot I was standing. The GPS was in her phone glove.

I turned back to the street and thought I caught sight of her heading up West Fourth Street, so I jumped the fence and ran. Surely if I returned her glove, she'd let me interview her. This girl would knock Speed sideways, I reckoned. I chased her all the way into the subway station.

I grabbed a MetroCard and took the stairs two at a time,

trying to keep her in sight. As I made it down to the platform the train doors were closing, so I long jumped, squeezing through, but got my backpack jammed. The train left the platform and I tried to force the doors apart, but they wouldn't budge. Then a guy with masses of black facial hair and a trench coat saw me struggling and shoved the doors open. I pulled my bag inside just as we disappeared into a long, dark tunnel.

"Thanks, man," I said, breathing hard, rubbing my ankle.

"No problem. Happens to me all the time."

I looked around the packed train car but couldn't see Melody anywhere. Was she even on this train? I started walking, searching the sea of faces. There was a guy eating a kebab, meat and sauce spilling down his chin onto the floor, a woman doing a puppet show that no one would look at, and rank body odor from random pits.

When we pulled into the next station, dozens of people poured out and in, and I hung my head through the door and scanned madly for Melody. I even called her name a few times, but people looked at me as though they wanted to beat me, so I kind of stopped doing that.

By the time I'd been through three cars I was thinking two things: (1) I was pretty sure she wasn't on the train, and (2) what the hell was I doing on it if she wasn't? Then, about five stops uptown, around 125th Street, I saw her. She was in the second-to-last car, reading a book, wedged between a

Rastafarian dude with dreads in a colorful woolen hat and a woman who looked suspiciously like a man.

I wanted to go up and give Melody the glove, but I was kind of curious about where she was going. I mean, why had she taken off so quickly when I asked her to talk about her inventions? I sat down at the other end of the car and watched her. Did this make me a stalker? I liked to think not. I wasn't a weirdo. Not really.

As I sat there, the train stammering along the tracks at lightning speed, I tried not to think about the fifty or so yards of concrete and soil above me, and then skyscrapers on top of that. I wasn't really sure why the tunnel didn't just collapse on us. To distract myself, I looked at the glove. It had a flexible screen and keypad sewn into the top of it. It was made out of stretchy black Lycra. I felt around to see where the battery was hidden, but there didn't seem to be one. I was tempted to play with it, but I held back. If I started hacking into the thing and got caught, I could kiss my Melody interview good-bye.

At 175th Street it seemed like we'd been on the A train forever. Where were we going? Canada? I started to worry. I'd figured we might only go a couple of stops, but now we'd been through eight. I pulled out my New York book. I had nothing on Manhattan this far north. Harlem was as far up as my book went. I hadn't even known there was anything up here.

I looked over toward Melody, and she wasn't there. I panicked and stood up, but then I realized she'd just changed seats.

I sat down again, wondering if I was nuts for doing this. Only the day before, we'd been chased by the skaters, and here I was, speeding up toward the Arctic Circle, following some peanut-butter-eating, graffiti-artist, inventor chick that I didn't even know.

Then there was a recorded announcement over scratchy speakers. "Last stop, Inwood–207th Street. This train makes no further stops. Last stop, Inwood."

Last stop? I thought. The handful of people still left in our car stood, ready to leave the train. Why had she come all the way up here? Maybe she'd *meant* to leave the glove in the restaurant so she could lure me up here, take me to an alley, and chop me up? Then again, there was always the chance that she lived here, I guess.

I decided I'd had enough. This stalking business was creeping me out. As the train pulled in and she got out I said, "Hey-y-y-y . . . Melody!" in my best "There you are! I've found you" voice.

She looked at me weirdly. "What are you doing here?"

I held up the glove.

"Oh my God. Thank you."

"You left it on the seat at the peanut butter place," I said.

"And you came all the way up here to give it to me?"

"Well . . ." I gave her my best "It was nothing" look.

"Thank you. I owe you one. And I'm sorry I left so quickly. I—"

"Forget it," I said. "It's cool."

"I was just thinking about you on the train."

The platform was empty now.

"Really?" I said, smiling. "What were you thinking?"

She pursed her lips. They were kind of nice.

"What?" I said, trying not to look at them.

"Can you keep a secret?" she asked.

"Me? Yeah, definitely. Why?"

"What were you saying before about being a coolhunter?"

"It's like a trend spotter," I said.

"I know what it is," she said.

"Well, you've got some cool stuff going on, and I—"

"But can you keep a secret?" she asked again. "Or are you always in coolhunter mode? I think I like creative, inventor Mac better than coolhunter-wanting-to-film-me Mac."

"Yeah, I think I do too," I said. "I can definitely keep my mouth shut."

She looked at me with those cute brown eyes. "Come with me. I want to show you something."

"What?" I said.

"You'll see," she said.

So I followed. We walked out of the station and over a couple of streets. It felt like a sketchy neighborhood, much lower-rent than where we'd got on the train in Greenwich Village. It didn't look like any other part of Manhattan I'd seen so far. Maybe we were in the Bronx?

"Where are we?" I asked her as we crossed a street and walked into a park that stretched into the distance for as far as I could see.

"Inwood," she said. "Some people call it Inweird 'cause of all the artists and stuff who live here now. It's a big Dominican neighborhood. You've got to try Dominican cheesy *pastelitos*. They're the best ever."

I followed her along a track through the park and up a hill.

"What do you want to show me here?" I asked.

She didn't answer, just kept on walking.

After five minutes or so, she said, "Not everyone is allowed to see what I'm going to show you, but I think we'll be okay. I think I should take you and just deal with the consequences."

"What consequences?" I asked her, trying to keep up.

"You'll see," she said. We were winding through a kind of wilderness now. It didn't even seem like we were in a city. We came to a fork and took the right-hand path, still winding upward. I tried to remember the turns.

Ten minutes in, I'd had enough of her little surprise. "I'd kind of like you to tell me where we're going now," I said, stopping.

She turned and smiled.

"Are you scared?" she asked.

"No, I'm not scared. I just don't want to keep walking up here until you tell me where we're going. I've got stuff to do today."

She looked at me and smiled. "You're scared," she said.

I knew I was sounding weird, but all I'd wanted was to interview her back at the peanut butter joint. I didn't want to marry her. Not yet, anyway. Not until I found out if she was going to chop me up.

"Trust me," she said. "Okay? It's not far. You'll be fine." And then she walked off. Now I knew how Paul felt with me telling him to "relax" all the time and to "just trust me." It was kind of annoying. I looked down the path and considered heading back to where we'd come from. But we'd taken a few different paths, there was no one around, and I wasn't so keen on stumbling for hours through a forest. Now I felt like I was *really* lost in New York.

So I charged on after her. A few minutes later we came to the top of the hill, where we could see right out over a river. On the other side were all these colorful trees. I could vaguely hear traffic in the distance, but there wasn't a building in sight.

"Native Americans used to live here," she said. "The Lenape, like the guy I painted downtown. They lived in those caves we passed." I remembered the rocks jutting out of the hillside.

"That's really great," I said. "Where are we?" But she took off and started winding down toward the river. I followed, and eventually a building came into view, a big boat shed built over the water.

"Is that where we're going?" I asked.

She didn't answer.

I tripped on some rocks, stumbled, and then regained my footing. I was staring through the trees, trying to get a good look at the boat shed and see if there were any goons hanging there, ready to take me out. Maybe she's part of a cult, I thought. And I'm their latest recruit. My mom had told me about a cult she got involved with when she was a teenager. I couldn't believe what a loser I was coming all the way up here. I tried to tell myself that Melody wasn't a psycho. But why wouldn't she just tell me where we were going? Maybe this was where they dumped bodies in Manhattan? Was I about to swim with the fishes? I wiped sweaty palms on jeans.

I'd told Paul to push boundaries and "be scary." What an idiot. Why didn't *I* make up a peanut allergy? He wasn't scared of life. He was scared of dying. That's why he wasn't being lured into some kind of weird death trap in the woods. Maybe now was the time to make a run for it?

We came to the water's edge next to the boat shed, where I could see a bridge to my left. It looked like the George Washington Bridge, which meant that this had to be the Hudson River and that was New Jersey on the other side. A bunch of boats steamed by. At least there'd be someone to find my body, I figured. All bloated and floating on the surface.

The shed was painted green and had moss and vines all over it. The gutters sagged with leaves. It was about as big as our school hall. Maybe bigger. There was no regular door that I could see. Just an old garage door covered in vines. Most of the shed was suspended over the water on wooden piers. It was a perfect mob hideout. Was this chick Mafia? Didn't I say she looked Italian?

"Hey, where'd you say your folks were from?" I asked her.

Melody pulled some branches away from a pile to reveal three little wooden canoes sitting on the riverbank next to the boat shed. She dragged two of the canoes into the shallows. This girl was strong. Then she handed me a paddle.

"What?" I said.

"Get in," she demanded.

"No way," I said. "Tell me where we're going. To the other side of the river?"

"No," she said. "Just round to the front. You enter from the water side."

"We're going in there?" I asked her.

"Yeah," she said, getting into the canoe.

"Not a chance," I said. "Look, thanks for the little nature walk. It's been fun, but there's no way I'm going to follow you into some old boat shed in the middle of nowhere."

A jogger ran past on the path that wound along the riverfront.

"This isn't the middle of nowhere. It's New York City!" she said.

But I wasn't going anywhere.

"Okay," she said. "I'll tell you. But it'll ruin the surprise."

The Hive

The side of my canoe bumped against the rotting wood of the old dock in front of the shed. Melody reached a hand down to pull me out of my boat. I took it, and the canoe lurched to the left, taking on water. I tried standing, and it wobbled dangerously. Then I lunged for the dock. Some rotting boards fell away as I landed on the deck, but I managed to stand. Melody tied the canoes to a pier covered in barnacles. The dock was a yard and a half wide, and it stretched about six yards out from the boat shed before the wooden boards fell away, collapsing into the river.

The boat shed looked even shabbier from this angle. Its peeling green paint was thick with black soot, probably from boat exhaust fumes.

"Now, just act normal," Melody said. "Like you're meant to be here. And if Joe Gatt comes up—he's a black guy, around six feet tall, kinda runs this place—let me handle him, okay?"

"Whatever you say," I said, and followed her along the jetty, dodging missing planks. Even though I'd demanded to know what was going on, all she'd said was that this was the Hive and that she knew I'd dig it. Somehow I'd bought that and jumped into the canoe. She just had this way about her.

Melody rapped on an old door—wooden panels stained with moss. The knock had a certain rhythm.

"That wasn't a secret knock, was it?" I asked her.

She smiled. *What kind of place has a secret knock?* My folks hadn't let me see many movies, but when I was a kid, my dad took me to a gangster movie double feature at the community hall. One was *The Godfather*, and the other I can't remember because I fell asleep during it. And something about this place said "Mafia." I was waiting for the door of the shed to swing open and for there to be a dozen guys called Paulie counting mountains of cash. I figured that pretty soon I'd be running jobs for them—'cause once you're in, you're in.

The door opened a crack, and we stepped inside. A young guy with dark, curly hair was holding it open for us.

"Hey, Jamie," Melody said, kissing him on both cheeks. "Thanks."

The door slammed shut behind us, and I took a few steps inside, then stopped and stared. The place wasn't gray and dingy with a single lightbulb hanging in the middle of the room. Far from it. It was clean. Superclean. It looked like Paul's mom had been at it. Only it had taste.

It was a big, open warehouse, painted white all over, with

exposed wooden beams in the ceiling and clear panels in the roof that let light flood into the room. There were stairs at the back leading up to a small, loftlike second floor. My eyes darted immediately toward a three-wheeled vehicle parked up there. It was silver with a curved roof and a front windshield that looked like it belonged on a fighter jet. It was maybe a quarter of the size of a regular car and beautifully sleek. It looked the way Paul and I always imagined the weird vehicles we created would look. But then we'd go and build them out of pieces of old scooters and junk from the scrapyard, and they always ended up looking ridiculous.

"Don't look up there," Melody said, dragging me by the arm.

"Why not?" I asked.

"Just don't," she said. "I'll show you everything else, but not that. Not now. And remember, if Joe gives us grief, leave him to me."

She led. I followed. I tried not to look up at the car, but it was hard. I felt as though, somehow, that machine was the reason I'd come to New York. I just had to figure out why. Melody glared at me again, and I diverted my eyes.

I noticed there was lots of old furniture all around the room. But it had been painted with big splashes of color—bright red desks, orange artwork, green light fixtures. Music was playing—an R & B track. I saw workbenches, people building things or writing, a girl painting on a canvas. And at the back of the building, written large on the wall, were the words CREATE OR DIE.

Everyone in the warehouse looked young. They buzzed about, working together at the ten or so workstations across the room. They all stared as we walked by, looking me up and down. Seemed like they weren't used to visitors around these parts.

A guy was sitting at a laptop on the far left-hand side of the building next to a window. The sun was shining in through gaps in the vines that hung outside, and the guy had what looked like a little solar panel plugged in to the AC adapter on his computer.

"Is that what I think it is?" I asked Melody once we'd gone by.

"Sure," she said. "There's no power in here apart from what we create. I've got a little wind-powered adapter, too, for when I'm out in the park."

We stopped at a desk in the corner at the back left-hand side of the warehouse, beneath the second floor. Melody picked up a small windmill from a bunch of stuff on a round white table.

"That's genius," I said. "Where'd you get it?"

"You know that guy we passed, Solomon, on the laptop?"

"Yeah."

"He built it for me."

"Is everyone here an inventor?" I asked.

There was a loud whirring sound and a massive bang from somewhere in the building. I hit the deck. It felt like a bomb had gone off. Little bits of black plastic scattered all over the floor, and a chunk of magnet landed not far from me.

There was a low, frustrated growl from the floor above.

I looked up at Melody. She was still standing. Then I looked around at the other guys. They were all on their feet too, most of them looking at me. No one had even batted an eyelid. Clearly it wasn't the first time this had happened.

Melody laughed as I peeled myself off the floor. "That was Joe," she said. "He's working on something that we're testing in a couple of days, but he keeps blowing it up."

"What is it?" I asked.

"Like I said, don't ask."

Her eyes flicked to someone behind me. I spun around.

Joe Gatt, I figured. He was a tall African-American dude with a shaved head, wearing a New York Yankees hat a little off center and a sensible-looking, short-sleeve checked shirt, light blue vest, and jeans. No shoes. Tattoos covered both arms. He must've been about nineteen, I guessed.

"Who's this?" he asked.

"This is . . . This is my friend Mac. He's an inventor. From Kings Bay," Melody said, coming to stand next to me as if we had more chance against him if we stood united. My mom would have described him as a very big presence. His back was dead straight. His eyes drilled a hole right through you.

"I don't care where he's from. I just want to know why he's here," Joe said forcefully.

"He's . . . Can we talk about this in private?" Melody asked.

Joe stared at me as Melody walked toward the stairs.

"Give me a second. Make yourself at home," she called.

Joe Gatt followed Melody. They disappeared upstairs, but he glared at me through the open staircase as he climbed.

I breathed out heavily. Who the hell was this guy? Why did he care so much that I was here? And did he destroy the whole car upstairs? I took a few steps out from beneath the second floor and looked up. It was still there. But what was it? I had a quick flash of me taking it for a spin, and I actually drooled a little. Was I some kind of animal with no control over my bodily functions?

I tried to take my mind off the car and looked around Melody's little corner of the warehouse. She had clippings and photos and bits of colored paper stuck to a bulletin board on the wall. There were quotes like "Creativity can transform the world" and "Make art, not war" and "The best way to have a good idea is to have lots of ideas." There was a *lot* of pink stuff. There were T-shirts on hangers with images like the one she'd painted on the wall downtown. Her desk had paint dripped all over it. The rollerballs were underneath. I scooched down to have a look, picking one up. It was heavy. I *so* wanted to take them for a ride.

I looked around to see if Melody was coming. She wasn't, so I had a look through the stuff on her desk. There was a thin, homemade-looking book called *The Swarm* by Joe Gatt, and

I saw a whole bunch of designs for clothing and gadgets. One in particular caught my eye. It was a sheet with four or five vehicle designs. One of them was identical to the thing up on the second floor. It had the word "Perpetual" written beneath it. To me it looked like a cross between a car and a motorbike. Two wheels at the front, one at the back. It wasn't like anything I'd seen before.

"Cupcake?" said a voice.

I let the papers drop to the desk.

Melody was standing behind me, holding a tray of cupcakes.

"No, I'm okay," I said, feeling guilty about rifling through her stuff.

"These are life-changing cupcakes," she said. "I made them yesterday afternoon, but they're still soft."

She offered them up.

"How old am I? Five?" I asked, grabbing a cupcake with blue icing.

She laughed.

"You get a good look at my work there?" she said, laying the tray on top of the papers I'd been looking at.

"Sorry," I said, guiltily taking a bite of cupcake.

"Good, huh?" she said.

They were. They were almost head-size-doughnut good.

"What's in these things?" I asked.

"Secret recipe," she said.

"Is everything a secret around here?" I asked.

"Almost," she said. "Now, I'm really embarrassed to say this, but Joe's kinda said you've got to leave. I thought he might be cool with you, but this is his place and—"

"Can you just tell me what this place is?" I asked. "What other stuff are people making here? Is this where you made the computer glove thing? And what about the skates? How do they work? I *need* to know."

Her eyes darted toward the stairs. No sign of Joe.

"I'll walk you out the long way. C'mon," she said, heading off toward the far side of the building. She spoke quietly.

"Joe's from Queens," she said. "He used to be a hip-hop promoter. Made a bucket of cash when he was, like, fourteen, but got sick of hustling. He wanted to get creative and work with artists, designers, inventors, engineers, writers. Kids with original ideas come here to develop stuff. We all work together."

"Is that why it's called the Hive? You guys are like bees?" I asked as we weaved our way through the workstations.

"Joe calls it swarm creativity," she said. "A group of minds is always smarter than the brightest person in the group. We're a swarm, like a mini-Internet. We solve problems together. It's the future, but it's happening now."

"And do you pay rent here, or . . . ?"

"It was abandoned. We're kind of looking after it for a while, rent free, if you know what I mean."

I looked back over my shoulder, up to the second floor.

Gatt was there, staring right at me. The three-wheeler was covered now. Why didn't they want me to see it? What was the big deal?

"Don't look at him," Melody said.

"Sorry."

"He's supertouchy right now. Like I said, this trial's in a couple days, and he gets edgy when things aren't going right."

I liked the way she said "couple days."

"What's that?" I said. We were walking past Jamie, the curly-haired kid who'd let us in. He was wearing a hat made of rubber and metal and standing in front of a TV. One second he was crying, and then he'd start laughing, and a second later he'd get angry and swear at the TV. The dude had problems.

"It's an anti-channel-surfing device. A TV that chooses the perfect show for you based on your mood. He's seeing if he can trick it by faking."

The guy burst into tears again, but the movie on-screen stayed the same.

"It's *High School Musical*," Melody said. "I can understand why he's crying."

"It's a cool idea. Is he gonna sell it?" I asked.

"There're only two rules here," she said. "One is that you can't sell or mass-produce anything you develop. One-off items only. The Hive's about stretching your creativity, not your bank balance."

"What's the other rule?" I asked.

We arrived at the door where we'd come in. We both looked up to the second floor, and Gatt motioned for Melody to get rid of me.

"We've got to hook up before you leave New York," she said. "But swear to me you won't say anything about this place, okay? That's the other rule: You don't talk about the Hive."

I was a coolhunter. This place was deeply cool. And she wanted me to keep quiet about it?

"How do I get involved?" I asked. "I'd love to work on something here, even if it's just for a few days. I'd love to talk shop with the rest of these guys. How do I get to stay? Maybe I can talk to Joe and—"

"You'd better go," she said. "Make sure you drag the canoe right up the bank and cover it up."

"Can you just tell me what the car thing is? Why's it called Perpetual?"

"I could tell you, but I'd have to kill you," she said, serious.

I looked at her.

"Kidding," she said. "Sort of."

"Please," I said. "I swear I won't say anything."

Melody bit her lip and looked behind her. Gatt had disappeared.

"Tell anyone, even your dog, and you're gone," she said.

"I don't have a dog," I said.

"You know what I mean."

"Scout's honor," I said.

"Are you a scout?" she asked, surprised.

"No."

"It's a perpetual motion machine," she whispered. "Now go!" She pushed the door open, I stepped out, and she slammed it shut.

I stood there for a second, staring at the door. A perpetual motion machine? Was she for real? Paul and I had tried to build one as a fourth-grade assignment, and we'd blown the thing up and burned a big hole in his bedroom carpet. Paul reckoned it was impossible to create an actual perpetual motion machine. It couldn't be done.

I jumped into a canoe and started paddling back to shore in a post-Hive daze. I thought about the skates, the glove, the weird anti-surfing device. And Perpetual. Part of me was desperate to be a Swarm member, to be accepted. The other part knew I had to hunt the Hive.

The Real world

"You're lying."

It was five in the afternoon, and we were in the downstairs lounge area of our hotel room. I'd hit Paul with the whole story, all in one stream. Marshmallow Fluff, the train ride, the park, the canoes, the Hive, Joe Gatt, the inventions, and Perpetual.

"Do you think I'm lying?" I asked.

"Well, it sounds like a lie, but then, you're not acting like you're lying. But even if you actually went to this place, the most exciting thing about it is the perpetual motion machine that blew up while you were there and, hello, we both know it's not possible to make one."

I was sitting on the couch, feet on the coffee table. Paul was pacing up and down in front of the giant glass windows, the sun getting low over the ocean of skyscrapers behind him.

"She reckons they're testing it in a couple of days, and I want to be there."

"Mac, it's not possible to create a machine that puts out more energy than you put in. Friction is always gonna slow it down. It defies the first law of thermodynamics!"

"I know, you've told me that, but if anyone ever does it, won't it, like, solve global warming or something?"

"Free fuel? Unlimited energy? Are you kidding me? It'll save the freakin' world!"

He was working himself into a frenzy now.

"Why wasn't I there?" he asked.

"Peanut allergy," I said.

"Ha ha."

"We *have* to put this up on the site," I told him.

My phone rang. It was Speed.

"But didn't she say you couldn't tell anyone?" Paul said.

I hit answer.

"Hello?"

"What up, guv?" Speed said.

"Hey," I said.

"What've you got for me?" he asked.

All I'd actually shot that day was a minute's footage in the peanut butter sandwich joint and the Tickle Shop, both of which now seemed way lame compared with the Hive.

"Well . . . ," I said.

"Yes?" He waited for me to go on.

I looked at Paul. "Can I give you a call back?" I said. "I'm just in the middle of something."

"Don't be long. I want to hear what you're putting up."

"Yeah, sure. I think it's gonna be good," I said.

I hung up.

"Did you shoot this Hive place?" Paul asked.

I looked at him.

"Nothing?" he said.

"No, but . . ."

"Well, that's probably good. It sounds like this Gatt dude would finish you. And the perpetual motion machine sounds cool, but it's not true and it's not worth dying for."

"We came to New York to hunt cool," I said. "I've just lifted the lid on the coolest thing ever. You think it could bust science wide open and save the world, and you're prepared to walk away?"

"But you said that's one of the rules: You don't talk about the Hive," he said.

"Rules, schmules. We're not being paid to keep promises. We're being paid to dish the goods."

"Are you for real?" Paul asked.

"I've been dreaming my whole life of coming to New York and making it somehow. I might never come back here, so this is my one shot, and I'm prepared to take some risks to make it happen."

"But—"

"I say we do, like, a video diary thing, talking about what we saw at the Hive."

"We?" Paul asked.

"Yes, 'we,'" I said.

"How about we put the Tickle Shop up instead?" Paul suggested.

"You hated the Tickle Shop!"

"It had a certain charm," he said.

"You really don't want to keep this job, do you?" I asked him. "You're desperate to be back hacking kebab meat off the rotisserie and cleaning the crispy bits out of the fryer at Taste Sensation."

"I just don't want these Hive guys chasing us with metal bars like the skater dudes. And didn't you say Gatt had tattoos?"

"Yes, but tattoos aren't alive. They can't hurt you," I said.

We argued for a while. Paul caved. I stuck my phone on top of a chest of drawers upstairs. Paul sat on the end of the bed, looking into the lens.

"You ready?" I asked.

"I guess."

"Just don't mention Perpetual or the name of the place, okay?" I said. "We'll be kind of vague on the details. It'll be fine."

I hit record and sat down next to him.

Me: We have just found the coolest thing in New York.

Paul: Yeah.

Me: Somewhere in the city, there's this group of kids who are inventors.

[I nudge Paul.]

Paul: Yeah, and they're creating all this stuff: new technology, clothes, ways to get around.

Me: *Incredible* ways to get around. It's way more cutting edge than anything you've seen. And they're our age! But the stuff they invent is just for them. They're only allowed to create one-offs. Which means you can't get it. But this stuff is awesome. Like the skates we saw.

Paul: Anyway, we're not giving too much away right now.

Me: But we will tell you they're working out of a warehouse somewhere in Manhattan. So stay tuned over the next few days. We'll be going undercover to bring you the best of the best from the Hive.

I got up to cut the camera.

"I thought you weren't supposed to say 'the Hive,'" Paul said.

"Oh, yeah, we'll cut that bit," I said. "Now let's upload. At least it'll take the heat off us for now."

So we did. I edited the piece in the phone and uploaded it to the site. Paul had made me feel slightly nervous, but what was the chance of anyone from the Hive being a Coolhunters subscriber? He forced me to stick the Tickle Shop up too. He was kind of hoping it'd be a bigger hit than the Hive vlog and we could leave Gatt and the Swarm alone.

At eleven, before we went to bed, we checked the site on

my phone. You usually had a pretty good idea if something was hot or not within the first few hours of putting it up. We checked the Tickler first.

Five people had watched it.

Then we scoped the numbers on the Hive teaser.

Seventeen thousand hits in five hours.

Speed had shot me a message.

good numbers, lads. but it's a big promise. when's the next installment?

tickle shop? horrible. dirty.

don't let me down. clock's ticking. you need to deliver on this promise tomorrow.

s

I logged out, turned to Paul, and said, "We're going back up there."

Return to
◁ the Hive ▷

It was 8:07 a.m., Sunday. We'd tried to Dawg Find Melody earlier, but her phone was off or she'd gone phantom, so we caught the subway. My dad came with us and jumped off near the Empire State Building. It gets struck by lightning a hundred times a year, and Dad figured he could learn something for his lightning farm back home.

The hit count on the Hive teaser was off the hook—up to forty-something-thousand overnight. We had hits from Iceland, Greece, Fiji, and Argentina. I couldn't believe that people wanted to watch something that didn't actually say anything. They didn't even know about Perpetual.

I sat there playing with the video functions on my phone. I was determined to shoot something that day at the Hive, even though Paul had other ideas.

"What if we want to *join* them, rather than cash in on them?" Paul asked.

"Okay, just say something," I said, pointing my phone at him. "I want to test the audio."

"Last stop, Inwood–207th Street," came the announcement over crusty speakers.

As I led the way up through Inwood Hill Park, the clouds seemed to crowd in not far above the tops of the trees. Paul stopped to read a plaque.

"Hey, says here that this was the main Manhattan Indian village and that some dude bought the island from the Native Americans for a bunch of trinkets and beads right here on this spot."

"Sounds like a good deal," I said sarcastically.

"For who?" he asked.

When we reached the view at the top of the hill, we stood for a minute and got our breath. It was Huck Finn country up there, or like the quiet parts in the hills around Kings Bay. Thick fog hung over the river. I couldn't even see the Jersey shore. We charged on downhill, and pretty soon the boat shed came into view. I put a hand out to slow Paul and scanned to see if there was anyone around before we continued down the hill.

I pulled the branches off two canoes and started dragging them to the shoreline. I was looking all around, along the waterfront and back up the hill, when I saw a flicker of red coming through the trees and down the path.

"Quick," I said, grabbing Paul and pulling him by the sweater up past the boat shed and behind some scraggly bushes on the waterfront. We sat there and watched. I waited for the person to jog right past, but he didn't. It was a tall guy with a checked shirt, a red vest, a shaved head, and a Yankees cap slightly off center.

"That's Joe Gatt," I said to Paul, heart thumping.

Gatt made it to the canoes and saw they were uncovered. He looked around, not happy. I pushed Paul's head lower.

"His tats are—"

"Sssshhh," I whispered.

Joe dragged one canoe up the bank, covered it, then jumped into the other. As he did, Paul's phone rang. Loud. Joe looked up. The ring went on and on as Paul wrestled it out of his pocket, my heart beating harder with every ring. When he finally had the phone out, rather than turn it off like any normal human, he answered it.

"Hey, Mom," he whispered.

I couldn't believe this guy.

"No, I'm in a library. Can I call you back later?"

A pause while he listened.

"Just doing some research," he said, and waited. I looked at him like I was ready to kill him.

"Yeah, we had eggs and stuff at the hotel."

I poked my fingers into my eyes, not believing what I was hearing.

"I have to go, Mom. Bye. Librarian's coming and he looks angry," he said, and hung up.

I peered out through the undergrowth. Gatt was gone.

I gave Paul a dead arm and took my first breath after what felt like about four minutes.

"Owwwww. Sorry," he said, grabbing his arm. "But she scares me more than he does. What do we do now?"

"We wait a minute and then we go in."

"Maybe we shouldn't," he said.

"Don't be a loser. I promise there are no peanuts in there."

"The guy's biceps are thicker than my legs," Paul said. "Maybe we should ask before we film in there? Like we should have asked at the half-pipe."

I didn't respond. I knew he was right, but I could hardly see Melody and Gatt throwing open their doors to us if they knew we were going to shoot. And we had a deadline.

We waited five minutes, jumped a canoe, and hit the dock. I gave "the knock."

Meet Joe Gatt

"You sure you got it right?" Paul asked.

"I dunno. Maybe not," I said. I was nervous as hell. It felt like only a few hours since I'd been chucked out of the Hive, and here I was, back again, working undercover this time. Was I an idiot? (Don't answer that.)

We were standing on the narrow wooden deck outside the boat shed. It had just started raining. A massive container ship cruised through the fog. We huddled in close to the building.

"Maybe knock louder," Paul said.

So I tried again to remember the knock.

We waited.

"Oh, well. No one home. Let's go," Paul said.

I was tempted to jump back in the canoe, when a bolt shifted on the other side of the door. It opened a crack, and Melody's face appeared.

"Hey-y-y-y," I said. "How you doin'?"

Melody squeezed through the gap. "What are you doing

here?" she said in a sharp whisper, pulling the door shut behind her. She glared at Paul.

"Coming to say hi," I said.

"Well, that's not okay," she said. "You should've called."

"Your phone was off."

"Well, it's really not all right for you to come here."

It felt bad being rejected by her.

"Really?" I said. "But you *made* me come here yesterday."

"I know. But I got in a lot of trouble. Joe's all freaky about new people coming at the moment. He's totally paranoid. You didn't tell this guy what I told you about the thing, did you?" she said, motioning to Paul.

"No," I lied. Man, I was really making a habit of this.

"Just call me next time, okay?" she said, backing up inside. "I'll meet you downtown before you leave."

"Hang on a sec," I said, jamming my hand in the door before it closed. "Let me talk to Joe. Paul and I are cool. You know that. We make stuff ourselves. And I told you, we can totally keep a secret."

Maybe this was what people were talking about when they said someone was a compulsive liar.

"We just want to be a part of this," I said. "I swear I can talk anyone into anything. Just let me speak to him. If he spins out, I'll tell him we forced our way in, threatened to bust your chops."

That made her laugh. "My chops?" she said, looking at me for a long moment. "Wait here a second."

I started rehearsing what I was going to say to Gatt. I'd kind of worked it out the night before, but now it was all mashed up inside my head.

Melody was back in under a minute. "Knock yourselves out," she said, opening the door for us.

We stepped inside. There weren't as many kids there as the day before. Seven or eight. A couple of them were covering up Perpetual on the second level. I caught a glimpse of the fighter jet front. I could see Joe Gatt sitting cross-legged up on the second floor. He looked like he was meditating.

Once Perpetual was covered, my eyes drifted around the Hive. It felt like a giant version of our workshop back in Kings Bay. Except ours had a dirt floor. And a smashed window. And it was kind of falling down. In fact, there weren't that many similarities. But both places smelled like good ideas. You could just feel there was something exciting going down there. I looked at Paul. He was standing slightly behind me, and I could see the words CREATE OR DIE reflected in his glasses. He had the same look that I'd had on my face the day before.

We followed Melody, making a beeline for the stairs. A few of the kids working on stuff looked at us as we went by. A Hispanic girl with yellow-framed glasses that I'd seen yesterday was painting gold birds on a giant red canvas. She smiled at us.

"Just wait here," Melody said when we reached the bottom of the stairs. She climbed the flight and disappeared. Paul and I looked around.

"What do you think?" I asked him.

"Is that a . . . ?"

At that moment a girl went soaring down a zip line from the second floor to the door where we'd come in. She pushed the door open and disappeared outside.

"What was that about?" Paul asked.

"Dunno. I call first dibs, though," I said.

"I'm second," Paul said quickly, as though there was someone else there who could have gotten in before him.

"Guys," Melody called from the top of the stairs.

I took a deep breath. "Good luck."

We made it to the top, and there was Gatt sitting on a yoga mat. I noticed he had tattoos on his knuckles, too. He was next to a desk with a computer screen so thin it was almost invisible. There was a small, transparent keyboard in front of the screen. It was on a white desk. There were neatly clipped images of futuristic-looking vehicles on a notice board. The CREATE OR DIE sign loomed large on the wall behind him.

"'Sup?" Joe asked, not opening his eyes.

"Baddha Konasana," I said. Paul frowned at me. Gatt opened his eyes.

"You do yoga?" he asked.

My mom taught a bit of yoga as well as fire twirling. Baddha

Konasana was one of the basic seated poses. I noticed that he wasn't really doing it right. *Should I tell him?* Before I thought about it, the words started pouring out.

"I think you've, um, got to tuck your heels into your groin a little more," I said, regretting it immediately. Gatt stared at me like he might show me those knuckle tats in close-up. But then he tried pulling his heels back.

"That workin' out okay for you?" he asked.

"Yeah," I said. "That's . . . better."

"Tell me what you want," he demanded.

I looked at Paul. Then I whispered to him, and he whispered back.

"We want to create a flying machine for kids," I said. "With clean fuel or none at all."

"No fuel?" he said.

Had I blown it that I knew about Perpetual?

"Yeah," I said. "A safe, solo flying machine for kids. We've almost done it, but it needs a little refinement. Well, a lot of refinement, but in a place like this I think we could do it, y'know. We're only in New York for a few days, but with help from people who think like us, maybe we can fast-track it. That's kind of our dream."

He stared at us. "Kind of?" he asked.

"Well, it *is* our dream," I said, trying to sound certain.

"Why flying?" he asked.

"Um, fun," I said. "Fast. Flying lets you understand stuff you don't learn on the ground. And there's all that space up there not being used. It just makes sense."

Gatt closed his eyes, breathed deeply.

"There's something I don't like about you," he said.

My heart sank.

I don't know what it is. . . . But I like your idea. It's big. I like big ideas."

My heart rose again.

"I don't want you here. Not now," he said. "But if Melody's gonna vouch for you . . ."

"Yeah," she said, then she had a long look at us and said, "Yeah, I'll vouch for them."

I'm glad she wasn't hooked up to a lie detector, because she was pretty unconvincing. Did we look that guilty?

"Look around," Gatt said. "See if anybody wants to talk to you. But remember, the second rule of the Hive is—"

"You don't talk about the Hive," I finished.

He opened his eyes again, irritated by my butting in. It was a bad habit of mine.

"Speak to anybody outside these walls about what's going on here and your life won't be worth living, *sí*?"

His biceps tensed when he said this.

I nodded. *"Sí."*

"They screw up, it's on your head," he said to Melody.

She nodded. My eyes flicked to CREATE OR DIE.

Melody smiled. Joe closed his eyes. The meeting was over.

As Melody led us to the stairs, Paul and I stared at the covered-up Perpetual and the tools lying on the floor all around it.

"Go near that and you're dead," Gatt said without opening his eyes.

Blastoff

The pilot squeezed the trigger, and two intense bursts of smoke shot from his jet pack. I hit record on my phone and looked around to make sure no one was watching me. I tried to act casual, like I wasn't filming anything.

The pilot was Heath—medium height, stocky build, sandy hair. We'd just been introduced, and he was standing on the dock outside the Hive, two cylinders attached to his back via an aluminium rig with grip handles out front. He wore a blue helmet with white clouds hand painted on either side.

"We tested thrust on some model rockets," Dan said in a slow southern accent, checking Heath's pack. Dan was Heath's inventing partner—tall, skinny, lots of acne. "And we've had two test flights that have gone pretty well."

"They've been developing it for nearly three years," Melody said.

"My father's in fuel, and he helped us work out how to run

it using cellulosic ethanol rather than fossil fuels," Heath said, pulling goggles down over his eyes.

"Aren't those plants, like, causing a food crisis?" I asked.

"Yeah, but this fuel uses the stuff that others throw away. It's a waste product. Anyway, we're still in test mode."

"Thanks for letting us watch," I said. Paul and I had been so delirious when we heard these guys had a jet pack that they offered to show us.

"We were gonna have another test soon anyways. You're good to go," Dan said, giving Heath a slap on the helmet. We all shuffled back along the jetty toward the Hive. Heath, the pilot, moved to the end of the dock, near where the planks were falling away into the river. He adjusted the throttle, giving the unit another quick blast. Seconds later, he gunned it and rose up off the jetty.

He shot directly out over the river, his feet hanging a yard or two over the surface as he flew. Then he rocketed upward, his movements jagged. He looked like he could fall out of the sky any minute. But he didn't. He flew around in staggered circles like a mosquito hunting for blood. You'd think everyone would go wild, cheering, once he had lift-off, but the audience on the dock was silent, waiting for him to lose control and plummet into the Hudson. After about thirty seconds, he turned and started shooting back toward us. He was coming in fast and looked like he was either going to pull up short of the platform or tear down the rest of the jetty.

I glanced at my phone screen, checking if I had Heath in shot. I did. I had my arms folded and nobody even knew I was filming.

I looked up again as Heath dropped a couple of yards really quickly. I thought it was all over, but then he landed a foot on the dock. He slammed another foot down, and it plunged right through the timber, showering splinters of rotted wood as he came running along the pier toward us.

I couldn't believe he'd landed the thing. Everybody lost it, cheering and clapping and rushing in to see if he was okay. Heath ripped up the leg of his jeans, and it looked like he had a pretty good cut on his ankle and calf from the wooden deck, but apart from that he seemed okay.

I stopped recording, and Paul came over to me.

"You get that?" he asked.

"Think so," I said, pocketing the phone. "Next."

◅ Rollerballs ▻

Trees whipped past in a blur. My helmet strap flapped furiously under my chin. I howled like I do whenever I'm on something moving ridiculously fast. My eyes watered as wind ripped into my face. I wished I had a wing attached. I'd easily have taken off. For a second I thought about the hard, rough pavement beneath me and how it might feel on my face if I fell right now, but even that thought couldn't slow me.

I was testing Melody's skates on a path through the park. The "wheels" were like bowling balls set into boots. "Just lean forward," Melody had said when I first stood up. So I did, and then I quickly leaned back and fell on my butt. This happened about eight times before I finally got a feel for them.

She said the skates worked like a Segway. All you had to do was lean forward and they'd start rolling. If you straightened up, the balancing technology inside the skate would slow you down. Unlike a Segway, though, these babies had no kooky handlebars and no governor—the thing that slowed you down when you went too fast. "So just take it easy," she'd said.

Yeah, right. I had my arms straight at my sides and was leaning forward like an Olympic ski jumper. I was holding my phone, filming on the run. I hit the bottom of the hill. Now it was dead-straight ground and I could feel the tiny electric motors inside the skate shoes driving me forward.

Melody was back at the starting point, up in the tree line. Paul was in front of me, filming on his phone. He was standing at the edge of the park, near a road, about sixty or seventy yards away. I had to think about braking. *Just straighten up.* That's what she'd said. Straighten up and stop. But I'd been leaning forward for so long now that it felt weird to tip back, as though the skates might just shoot out from beneath me again. I gave myself a count.

"Three, two, one . . ."

Then I started to lean back. Just easing it.

I was leaning, straightening up. But the skates weren't slowing. They went right on careering toward the edge of the park. I tried turning one skate behind and dragging a foot like you do to slow down on regular blades. But because the wheels were big balls, I just kept rolling forward.

I was maybe twenty-five yards from the road now. I'd been in situations like this dozens of times. Flying bikes, kite-sk8boards and plenty of sketchy Mac-Paul inventions. I started to look for soft places to land, but if I veered off the path and onto the grass now, I'd break my neck. I'd jumped off enough skateboards at high speed to know that inertia's a killer. So what was I supposed to do? Skate onto the road? Hope there were no cars? Maybe.

Just then a bus pulled up on the road at the end of the path. At least there'd be something to stop me, I thought. I had a snap vision of those crash-test-dummy trials on badly made cars. The thing hits a wall and the dummies go flying through the front windshield and shatter into a thousand pieces.

Paul was still filming as I came speeding toward him.

"Help!" I called to him.

"Brake!" he said.

"Keep shooting!" I screamed, and I stopped those skates the only way I knew how.

Maybe There Is

I veered off the path and hit the grass at what must have been thirty miles per hour. I prepared for the roll. When the skates bit into the grass, they tried to throw me through the air, but I ducked my head, covered my face, rolled into the fetal position, and cannonballed along the ground, top speed. The trees were upside down, the sky was my floor, the grass was on the ceiling, and, when I stopped, body sprawled, every bit of me grazed and hurting, the skates were still spinning.

I moved my fingers gently, feeling the pain, then I lifted my head. My neck killed. I sat up slowly and rolled my shoulders around. Then I opened my eyes. Paul was above me, still filming.

"You okay?" he said casually.

"Yeah," I groaned. "How'd it look?"

"Venezuela, man," he said.

Paul had this thing about Venezuela recently. If something was cool, it was Venezuela. Go figure.

"She's coming," he said, cutting the camera and sticking it in his pocket.

We headed back to the Hive (they walked, I limped), and Melody and Paul cracked open the skates and tried to work out what had gone wrong. I zoned out when they started talking propulsion, stabilization, and gyroscopic sensors. Science was strictly Paul's area. I'd heard him say, more than once, "Physics is fun." He'd been known to download past exams for high school physics off the web and do them at home, for kicks. And I hung out with this guy.

I took a look upstairs, where Gatt was working on Perpetual with a girl and another dude. Gatt was smiling. The girl with him, who was maybe part Japanese, slammed the cover on the engine at the back of the machine. Gatt went back to his desk, the other two covered up Perpetual, and I headed back to where Paul and Melody were working. While they talked tech jive, I sat there trying to work out how we could get a closer look at Perpetual, see if it really was a perpetual motion machine before the trial went down. I wanted to shoot the test, but what was the point if it was a fake?

After a while, Paul and Melody cracked the skate problem. Paul was pretty proud of his input. The two of us went for a walk around the Hive. They were a weird bunch. Good weird. Not bad weird like some of the Coolhunters kids. We found this tall guy with superwhite skin. Albino, maybe. He looked like he was about twelve or thirteen. He was attaching little electrodes to the head of another guy, a redhead, who was lying on a torn single mattress on the floor. The electrodes were connected to a laptop through a series of red and green wires. The computer had USB solar, powered by light from the clear roof panels above.

"Hey," I said.

"Fiddle-dee-dee, neighbor," he replied.

"I'm Mac. This is Paul."

"I know," he said. "Mel told me. They mostly call me Dink."

He went over to the computer and typed for a second.

"You mind telling me what you're working on?" I asked him.

"This here's a mind mapper."

"What's that?" Paul asked.

"Also called a dream machine," he said. "It's a way of recording people's dreams on video."

"No way," I said.

"Yes way," Dink said. "It turns an EEG, which records electrical activity in the brain, into images."

"That's incredible," I said.

"It would be," he said. "If it worked. EEG machines cost a ton, and my homemade app doesn't quite cut it. I'm starting to think of it more as an art installation than a scientific breakthrough." He laughed, baring big teeth and bright pink gums.

"Okay, just listen to the music, relax. Let yourself sleep," he said to the guy on the mattress.

Dink leaned over to me and whispered, "My last invention was a materializer, which let you download solid objects from the web. Like books and skateboards and stuff."

"No way!" I said.

"Didn't work either," he whispered. "I'm having a bad run."

Paul and I hung there for a while. There was a bit of static on the computer screen at one stage, but that was about as exciting as it got.

"See you 'round," I whispered.

Paul picked his phone up off the desk and clicked stop as we moved on. "I hate doing this," he said, keeping his voice low. "I feel like a thief."

So did I, but I didn't see that we had a choice. We needed something to feed Speed. Our other option was to forget about coolhunting altogether and go back to our regular lives, but I just wasn't ready to do that yet.

We found a chick called Hannah who was writing a novel on her cell phone and giving away chapters for free every day on the web. It was written in short, sharp bursts of a hundred words. She was writing it with Oscar, a guy who sat across the desk from her. They'd write a chapter each and send it to the other writer, who'd react with the next chapter. Sometimes the chapters had video embedded, other times just still pics. Joe Gatt was cool with it, apparently, because they were giving it away and weren't mass-producing anything.

"I'm getting ready to go," Melody said, coming up behind us. She and Hannah hugged.

My eyes went to Melody's feet. "What are they?" I asked her. At first it'd looked like her feet were bare, but then I realized she was wearing some kind of clear shoe.

"Oh, they're my UnSneaks," she said. "They're so old."

I knelt down on the ground and looked at them, close up. I didn't even care that much about clothes and shoes, but these things were cool. Clear sneakers. Invisible sneakers, almost. Kind of homemade looking when you got close, which made them seem even cooler.

"I like having bare feet," she said, "but you can't exactly wear no shoes in New York, so I made UnSneaks. They feel like bare feet too. Everybody helped me make them, but these are the only pair. They're *so* comfortable, but they stink. We forgot about ventilation. Don't get too close."

I looked up at Paul and noticed he was holding his phone at a weird angle. It was trained on the UnSneaks. I felt a pang of guilt that he was filming them, but I knew these things were hot.

"Guys, I'm leaving. You ready?" Melody said.

I looked at my phone. It was after two. No wonder I was hungry. The Hivers were starting to drift out the door.

"Sure," I said, standing and looking upstairs. "Hey, is Joe still here?"

"Don't," she said, and pushed me toward the door.

"But how would he ever know?" I complained.

"Believe me, he'll know. He knows everything."

"Just a peek at the engine," I said.

"He would kill me. Seriously," she said. "I got school tomorrow, so I won't be around. Not till late. Trial's tomorrow night."

"Really?" I said. "Could we come, 'cause—"

"I'll ask him," Melody said as she shoved open the door and we stepped outside. There was a cold breeze coming off the river. "But don't hold your breath."

"Where's it happening?"

"Bet you'd love to know," she said, heading off along the dock.

"Do you really believe it's a perpetual motion machine?" Paul asked her. "Like, really?"

"I know it is," she said without turning around. "I saw it working this morning before you guys invited yourselves in. That's why Joe was in such a good mood."

"That was a good mood?" I said.

"Was for Joe," she said.

"Who is this guy?" I asked. "I want to know more about him. Why's he so hard-core on the anti-consumer thing? Why so paranoid?"

She started climbing down off the dock into a canoe. There was only one tied up.

"He knows who he is. He's not trying to impress anybody else. And he's not prepared to sell out," Melody said.

I wondered if this was directed at me. Was she saying I was a sellout?

"Joe's dad used to tell him how lots of the world's great inventions have been turned to military use. Humans can't help themselves. He's not prepared to let that happen with perpetual motion," Melody said. "I'll bring back the other boats."

"But what if the trial works?" Paul asked. "What's he gonna do? Keep it to himself? Just in case someone chooses to do something bad with it?"

Melody shrugged, standing in the canoe, looking back up at him. "I guess. Hey, I thought Mac didn't tell you about it."

"Sorry," I said.

"That's insane!" Paul went on. "If it's a perpetual motion machine—which it isn't, but say it actually is—then a bunch of kids have achieved what some of the world's greatest scientists never have. And he's going to give up the chance to eliminate the need for fuel, maybe save the planet, just because he doesn't want to sell the idea? Why doesn't he just give it away?"

Melody untied the rope and sat down in the canoe, grabbing an oar.

"Once he's conquered an idea, he's not interested in exploiting it."

"Well, he *needs* to be interested this time," Paul said.

"I know, but he's Joe. He doesn't change his mind. Forget about it. There's nothing we can do."

She started paddling toward shore.

"You know what?" I called. She turned. "Maybe there is."

undercover

"Here's how it goes down," I said to Melody as she bumped into the dock, dragging the other two canoes behind. "Paul and I shoot the trial undercover, we show Joe the footage afterward, and we let him decide if he wants to tell the world."

She handed me up a paddle.

"Just get in the boat," she said.

"No," I said.

"Whatever. Do what you want, Mac, but I'm not listening to you." She slid two paddles onto the dock, sat back in her boat, and used her oar to push off from the pier. She started paddling for shore.

"Just listen to us!" Paul shouted at her.

Melody stopped paddling and looked up. She was as surprised as I was by Paul's random act of rage.

"Are you really going to turn your back on this?" he asked her. "What if I'm wrong? What if this Gatt dude's cracked it? You seem to think he has, and if he's done it, you've got no choice but to get him to tell people about it."

Melody was about ten yards away from the dock now, drifting toward the shore, not paddling in either direction. I figured this was our last shot at convincing her.

"He might not want to talk about it before the trial, but what if he pulls it off, a world first, and we have video evidence of it?" I asked her. "Once he watches it, maybe he'll change his mind."

Even as I said it, I didn't know if I actually cared whether people knew about Gatt's world-changing invention or if I just wanted to be the hero who uncovered it.

Melody stared into the bottom of the canoe for a long moment. Then she dug an oar into the water.

⊲ Perpetual ⊳

Melody spun the rotor, and the machine began to move, slowly at first, but then it gathered pace. Paul and I looked at each other. This was it. But, after about ten seconds, it died. She turned it again, but nothing happened.

"It was working this morning," she said quietly.

There was a sound from downstairs and we all froze, staring at the door. Melody's face went white with fear. We crept around so that the car was between us and the door. The three of us sat and waited.

It was just after 5:00 p.m., and we were on the second level at the Hive. We'd come back inside, waited till everybody left, and then climbed the stairs.

We didn't hear the noise again, so we moved back around to the engine.

"I can't believe I'm doing this," she said, adjusting some magnets on the complex-looking engine at the back of Perpetual. "This is so bad."

"It's not bad," I said. "We're gonna ask for permission. Just not now."

Paul and I had convinced Melody that we needed to shoot the test, and Paul told her that if we were going to shoot the test, we needed to shoot the engine first. We had to have evidence that it was a perpetual motion machine. Otherwise it'd be written off as another online scam job.

The deal was win-win. We'd get the scoop of the century, Gatt would save the world. Bada-bing, bada-boom.

Melody spun the rotor again. It began to pick up pace and was looking hopeful. But then it slowed again to a stop.

"I don't think we have to worry about Gatt finding out," Paul said, hitting stop on his camera phone. "We're not gonna waste our time shooting something that doesn't work."

"Shut up," Melody said. "You want to see the thing or not? I've never started it myself before. I designed the body of the car, but the engine was all Joe."

I shot Paul a look.

The engine had what looked like an electric motor at one end, then there was a shaft connected to a wheel with magnets stuck to it. The magnets passed by a coil made out of wire, which apparently created electrical energy. A simple generator.

"I've got to overload the electric engine," Melody mumbled as she played with both ends of the machine, "which somehow causes magnetic friction to be turned into a magnetic boost. Then the engine *should* just keep spinning faster and faster.

That's why the magnets flew all over the place during the tests. Slowing the thing down is harder than making it go."

"And braking is what recharges the engine?" Paul asked, starting to film again.

"In theory," she said. "It's something to do with rotating magnetic fields. I don't think even Joe fully understands why it works, but it does."

Then she gave it another spin, and this time, the machine started gaining pace, speeding up soundlessly until the magnetic rotor was just a blur. As it continued to speed I started to worry that it was going to spit magnets again. I stepped back a little. So did the others. The machine kept on turning.

Paul's eyes sprang wide open. He was gazing at it like a surfer might look at an incredible swell or a BASE jumper might stare at an outrageous cliff face they dreamed of jumping off. I loved moving fast, but for Paul it was all about how things work. Our flying bike was cool, but perpetual motion had never been done. Ever. Anywhere. He moved in with the phone-cam and shot a few things in close-up. Melody looked anxious as he did. Paul got down and listened to the engine, studied the drive shaft. Then Melody hit something, and it came to a stop.

"Show's over. We've got to get out of here."

Melody slammed the hood of the machine, and I went around and took a quick look inside the driver's cab before she covered the machine up again. It was pretty small in there.

Nothing like the inside of a regular car. Bare metal with just a steering wheel, a plastic seat, a couple of gauges for speed and revs. It wasn't so far off one of our prototypes after all.

I wanted to climb in and drive it so bad. "Can I just—"

"No," she snipped.

"Sorry. Hey, what's that?" I asked, pointing to a device on the dash.

Melody looked inside. "It sends out a high-frequency signal to a receiver at the traffic lights," she said. "Same technology emergency vehicles have on board. Jamie's dad is an ambulance driver and hooked us up. Supposed to give us green lights all the way."

"Road test, huh? How you gonna get it down from here?" I asked.

"Ramp, then out the garage door on the park side. Now get out of here," Melody snapped, throwing the cover sheet over the car and playing with the edges to get it exactly as Joe had left it.

"Test starts at the corner of West 218th and Broadway, two blocks downtown from the hospital, midnight tomorrow," Melody said as Paul went downstairs and I finished helping her with the cover sheet. "He's gonna ride Broadway the length of the island, north to south. Be there early and hide. And, whatever you do, don't get caught."

She didn't seem happy.

"Look, if you don't want to do this . . . ," I said, taking her hand. I don't know why I did it, but I did. Her skin felt good. Maybe I was a loser like Paul said, a freak who falls in love with every girl I meet.

"No, no. I do, I do," she said, leaving her hand there. "But you can't say anything about this to *anyone* till we speak to Joe and show him the footage after the test, okay? This is his invention, and he makes the call."

"Yeah," I said. We were standing only a few inches apart. Paul had disappeared downstairs.

"You go home the day after tomorrow," she said.

"Yeah. Thanks for doing this," I said.

"That's okay," she said softly, still full of nerves. "Like you said, people should know."

She looked me in the eyes, and I wanted to lean over right there and kiss her, but I had a flash of Jewels, my maybe-girlfriend back in Kings.

"You coming down?" Paul called.

"Yeah," Melody said. She looked back to me, pulled her hand away, smiled, and headed downstairs. I stood there, watching her go. Then I followed her down, across the Hive, and through the door to the outside, where she stopped on the dock.

"If Joe finds out about this before the test, he'll tear us apart. All of us."

"Got it," Paul said.

"Hey, one more thing . . . ," I said.

Melody looked at me.

"We sort of filmed me crashing the rollerballs today," I said. "You mind if we put it on the Coolhunters site tonight? We've kind of got to have something to—"

"Mac?" she said.

"Yeah?"

"I'm helping you with Perpetual because I think it's important. It's not an open invitation to exploit everything here, okay?"

Sliced Emu and Gut Worms

"The emu carpaccio?" said the waiter.

"Jubbly. Here, please," said Speed.

He'd taken us to one of his fave New York restaurants. An Aussie place in the heart of Midtown serving fish and chips, kangaroo satay sticks, and emu. It was one of about eight Australian joints that had sprung up all over the city. New Yorkers were knocking back meat pies on street corners like they were hot dogs or pretzels.

The waiter laid a plateful of bloodred, uncooked slices of emu in front of Speed. Around the table Michiko, Rash, Van, Luca, and Tony were getting their meals too.

"How'd you lads go today? Get some good stuff?" Speed asked, picking up a slice with his fingers and dipping it in sauce. He'd made a special request that Paul and I sit next to him so we could "have a little talk."

Paul and I looked at each other.

"Got anything on these teen Einsteins you promised us?" Speed said.

"Well . . . ," I said.

"Yeah?" he asked, a piece of raw emu stuck in the tuft of hair under his bottom lip.

"Tim Tam Tiramisu?" the waiter interrupted.

"Here, please." I wasn't much in the mood for eating, so I'd just ordered dessert. "We've got something big lined up for tomorrow night."

"What is it?" Speed asked.

"Can't tell you," I said.

"'Course you can."

"No, I can't."

"Don't play games, Mac," he said.

"I'm not meaning to. I just promised the person who promised us the thing for tomorrow that we wouldn't say anything."

Speed shook his head. "And what about today? I don't really care about tomorrow anyway, to be honest. Tomorrow is, like, fifteen years away. Our subscribers want it today or not at all. What have you got today?"

I looked down at my untouched tiramisu. We were stuck. We'd promised not to put the rollerballs on the site and that we wouldn't tell a soul about tomorrow night.

"This thing tomorrow'll be so hot if—"

"Look, I don't know what's going on with you two, but

you have one more day here and the best thing we've had from you is the promise of something that it appears you can't deliver. I told you guys that this is not an expenses-paid holiday."

"We just didn't really see anything cool today," Paul said.

"What? In all of New York, you didn't find a single thing you like? Mac, you?"

I shook my head. I tried to look him in the eyes, but I was probably staring more at his cheek.

Speed polished off the last slice of his tall, three-toed bird.

"Well, if you can't find cool in New York, then there's something seriously wrong with you."

That hurt. Especially when I knew we'd found the coolest thing in the world.

"But I think you're lying to me," Speed went on. "I know you've got something."

"We'll deliver tomorrow," Paul said.

"I took a chance on you guys, brought you out to New York. You lost a five-grand camera on the first day, and while everybody else has been coming up with brilliant stuff, you guys have delivered nothing. If you don't deliver tonight, there won't be a tomorrow. You can pack your bags."

Speed wiped Australia's national bird off his chin with a napkin and stood. "I have to use the men's room."

I could tell the other hunters were listening. I caught Michiko looking our way, grinning like she'd just won something. Van was staring at us through eyes smeared with bright pink and purple eyeshadow.

"We'll deliver tonight," I called to Speed as he headed off through the restaurant.

He didn't turn back.

Paul and I stepped outside. People raced by under black umbrellas as the rain poured. We huddled under the awning.

"Isn't this supposed to be spring or something?" Paul called over the sound of traffic speeding by.

"You want to make a run, get a cab?" I said.

"Mm," Paul grunted.

We were about to go for it, when the door opened behind us. I turned. It was Van.

"Hey," I said.

She closed the door and stepped in under the awning with us.

"I wanted to talk to you," she said.

I was immediately suspicious. Paul looked knives at her.

"About Speed."

"Yeah?" I said.

"Just watch out for him," she said. "I've been doing this longer than anyone in that room, and he's tried to pressure me like that plenty of times."

"So . . . ," I said.

"So, just be careful. He's a gut worm. He'll use you and spit you out. You don't know half the stuff he does with the information we give him."

"Like what?" I asked as a group went by laughing, raincoats on heads. Then Speed and the others pushed through the restaurant doors.

"Just watch out," Van said as she popped her umbrella, stepped out into the rain, and headed down Thirty-eighth Street with the group.

Upload or Die

Paul whipped me with a horsey bite, and I returned fire by grabbing his ears and pulling them very hard. He gave me a double nipple-cripple and I screamed, trying to detach his fingers, which were tearing my three or four chest hairs out of their sockets and possibly ripping my nips off too.

"Quiet!" Dad called from downstairs.

I silently tried to pry Paul's fingers away, but they were locked like a pit bull's jaw.

"Okay!" I said.

"Okay, what?" Paul asked.

"I won't put it up," I said, almost fighting back tears.

Paul released the pressure, and I lifted my shirt to check the damage. The hairs were gone and I'd swear he'd drawn blood.

I gave him a shove and wandered over to the other side of the room, pretending to tend to my wounds. Then I grabbed my phone off the floor, where Paul had levered it out of my hand, and I hit upload. Paul saw what I'd done and lunged toward me again.

See, he'd come upstairs and caught me cutting together the UnSneaks piece. Not that there was much to cut. It was just a minute or so of footage that Paul had filmed with Melody's explanation of the Sneaks serving as a voice-over. Even though the shooting was rough, the shoes looked cool.

Paul hadn't wanted me to upload it to the site. He said it was wrong. Like I didn't know that. But, like Speed said, if we didn't put something up, there would be no tomorrow for us. We didn't have a choice. I'd looked through all the other footage from the day, but not much of it was usable. So it was either me crashing the rollerballs or Melody modeling the UnSneaks. And she'd specifically told us not to upload the rollerballs.

Paul landed on me, and we slammed into the wall with such force that I felt the drywall give way behind me. Paul rolled off, and we both stared at the giant dent. The wallpaper was crumpled, and there were chunks of chalky stuff on the carpet.

"Nice one!" I spat at him.

"You heard what that Van chick said about Speed," Paul said, dusting plaster off his shoulder.

"What about it?"

"He's a gut worm. We knew that from the beginning. Why are you trying so hard to please him? The guy's using us," he said.

"What for?"

"I don't know. Coolness?"

"Yeah . . . like, we're so cool," I said. "Van's just saying that so we don't upload anything tonight. She's playing us."

"Well, it didn't sound like she was playing us."

I stood and headed for the shower.

"Melody's gonna hate you," Paul said.

I didn't have a comeback. I shut the bathroom door and cranked the hot water. Staring out at the lights of Manhattan through the full-length glass walls, I wondered if anyone could see me there, nude in the shower, or if it really was one-way glass like they said in the hotel info. I jumped out and grabbed a towel just in case. Never know when the coolhunter paparazzi might start chasing us.

My eyes were stinging. It had been the best and worst day of the trip so far. Best because we were semiaccepted into the Hive and got to do and see so much cool stuff. Best because of those few minutes on the second level of the Hive with Melody. Worst because of the pressure that Speed was piling on, to deliver no matter what.

I already wished I hadn't uploaded the shoes.

Around midnight, just before I switched off the light, I grabbed my phone and checked the Coolhunters site. We'd already had a few thousand views of the sneaks. It was going to be a hit. There were a bunch of comments:

Oh, my God. Get me a pair NOW! But I'll need an operation.
My toes are so ugly.
—Min, L.A., USA

at work and trying to forget about these shoes but i cant think
straight. yum!
—Sophie, Perth, Australia

I thort u guys had more depth than sneaker ads. least
homemade I guess.
—PhatFrog, Lisbon, Portugal.

The only pair? I don't even like them and I want them. Anyone
got ideas where these dudes' hideout is?
—MixRod, Wellington, NZ.

I tried going to sleep, but all I could do was lie there, lights from the city below shifting and drifting across the ceiling above me. At about one o'clock I sat up and grabbed my phone again and logged in to my blog, my private one.

im angry @ paul and melody. why don't they understand what
im trying 2 do here? i came 2 this city to find the coolest stuff
there is. i tap a bunch of way-cool stuff and im told i cant put
it on the web. why not? if someone wanted to report on one of
my inventions i'd be like "right on." if i talked to my ma about

this i know she'd dig joe gatt's decision not to sell out but what the hell? the guy is on the cusp of something massive 4 the world and without us it'd never see the light of day. and what does it matter that mel's unsneaks are being seen on the web? what diff will it make to her? none. i know it's not so cool to ask someone + get a no + then upload it anyway, but she'll understand. and what was i s'posed 2 do with speed all over us? it was upload or die.

I tried calling Melody, but her phone was still off. Then I googled **Joe Gatt**. There was nothing on him.

⊲ Trend Spotters ⊳

"I once, like, totally puked because my parents cut Internet access on my phone."

Paul and I were on the streets in the Tribeca 'hood, interviewing kids at bus stops, outside schools, in cafés, on the front steps of their apartment buildings—wherever we could get them. We had to wait till midnight for the Perpetual trial, and we needed backup material in case the machine exploded or Gatt finished us. We were asking about the little things we'd noticed as we were cruising around the city. Like the fact that kids as young as four had cell phones and were texting.

"I feel, like, almost dead without my cell phone. I get so mad at my mom when she takes it away from me. It's like taping my mouth so I can't speak." A seven-year-old girl eating breakfast at Starbucks.

"I watch Nick Jr. on my phone on my way to school," said a six-year-old kid waiting at the bus stop with his dad. "And sometimes, on my way home, I watch MTV. I like Madonna. She's old, but hot."

Every now and then, I'd check my phone for UnSneaks viewer numbers. Already over fifty thousand. People were going nuts for them. Melody's phone was still off.

As we cruised the city we discovered a thumb-wrestling trend too. Tons of kids with little homemade wrestling character thumb puppets playing Thumb Puppet Smackdown.

"We have a tournament running with around sixty wrestlers. I'm in fourth," said a kid with flame red hair as he wrestled his friend outside a subway station. "Ohhhhhhhhhh. Doctor Death crushes Toilet Head with a facebuster," he screamed as his thumb mashed the other guy into the palm of his hand, tearing the character's head off.

"Hey, no fair. Illegal move!"

I got down at eye level with the wrestlers and filmed a few rounds. I could imagine this going up on the Coolhunters site and dudes in offices thumb wrestling at the watercooler. And you could totally thumb wrestle in class and not get caught.

Another New York thing we discovered was the Caffeine Fiends—kids everywhere drinking coffee.

"I have a Honey-Soy MochaLatteFrappuccino topped with whipped cream," said an eight-year-old girl named Bridget with sticky-outty pigtails.

"Is that, like, decaf?" said Paul, looking up from his phone screen.

"No, caf," she said. "I one hundred percent could *not* stay awake at school if I had decaf."

Her mom looked on and shrugged her shoulders. "Kids," she said.

Where Paul and I came from, you didn't start drinking coffee in primary school. Matter of fact, I only knew about three people who drank coffee at my high school. Was I a pathetic small-town kook, or were these kids weird?

On the flip side of the Caffeine Fiends were the Sleepers.

"My folks are chronic," said a girl with messy blond hair who we found stand-up sleeping at a bus stop on Thirty-second Street. "My mom and dad drink, like, nineteen cups of coffee a day and they get, like, four hours' sleep a night, max, so they can spend more time trying to take over the world. But I sleep anywhere I can. It totally annoys them, and I love it. They say I'm lazy, but I'm just being a person."

"How much sleep do you get a day?" I asked her.

"About fourteen hours if I can. But some of it's just to mess with my parents' heads."

Once we'd been alerted to them, we discovered Sleepers everywhere. Hundreds, maybe thousands, of them. Asleep on buses, in the park, serving at hot dog stands. I'm pretty sure I saw a courier ride past on a bike with his eyes closed.

In Central Park after school we found about nine high school Sleepers curled up on the grass.

"We sleep just about anywhere we can," said a girl named

Hannah, who was about fifteen. She was jawing on a big yellow pacifier hanging from the side of her mouth. "There are Sleeper groups everywhere. We have sister cells in Brooklyn, Queens, and Staten Island, and sometimes we just get together and sleep in one big group."

"Sleep is so rock 'n' roll right now," said a twenty-year-old music video director we found sleeping on a bus with a copy of *Rolling Stone* over his face. "Sleep is the new awake. By the end of this year they're gonna be sleepin' in malls in Oklahoma. I just shot a music video with a major rap act—whose name I cannot mention—where he's asleep the whole way through. Kids are gonna break out in a rash over it."

Then it just became ridiculous. Suddenly it seemed like almost nobody in New York was awake. Businesswomen, artists, old ladies, cabdrivers waiting for a fare, homeless people on benches, a bunch of firefighters in deck chairs in the garage of a fire station, a judge wearing his wig on the steps of a courthouse. It made me wonder, was New York the city that never wakes up?

And here's something weird: People in New York *pay* for sleep. We took a ride up the Empire State Building to check this place called MetroNaps, where you pay to go to sleep for twenty minutes in an energy pod—a white, shiny spaceship for one.

"Sleep is my religion," said a guy in a suit coming out of there.

We were done filming by about three that afternoon and realized we hadn't stopped for lunch. Paul grabbed a hot dog, and I got a Not Dog (veggie version) from a guy with a cart on the corner of Central Park. We wanted them stacked high with sauerkraut, onions, sauce, mustard—whatever they could throw at us—but the dude told us that toppings were so Chicago. "The quintessential New York dog," he told us, "is very simple. Maybe a little kraut, some brown mustard, but they don't need either. Sometimes you just savor the dog in a bun. That's it." So we sat on the front of a fountain, ate the best hot/Not dogs in the world, and watched New York go by.

"I can't believe this place will still be here tomorrow afternoon but we won't," I said. Our flight was scheduled to leave at nine the next morning.

That's when my phone beeped. I felt sick already. I wrapped my dog and picked up the phone. I knew it was going to be Melody.

i saw my sneaks on yr site. u lied 2 me. u betta run. joe knows about it. if he finds u youre gone.

I exited the message, flicked to Dawg Finder, and clicked on Melody's icon. It was flashing up in Inweird. On 209th Street. I pressed delete, and it asked me if I wanted to delete this Dawg permanently. I thought about it for a long moment and decided there was no way I could have Gatt finding us. I hit yes and her icon disappeared. My map was empty.

Me vs. the City

We walked silently back from the subway station to the hotel. I packed my bag while Paul played soccer on the big screen. Dad slept. We ordered food up to the room, and I sat on the floor next to the piano and looked down at the traffic below while I ate. All I could think about was Melody's text, wondering why I did what I did, uploading those sneaks. At about ten thirty I started blogging on my phone.

hey. i'm depressed. if I hadn't uploaded those sneaks we would have lost our jobs but I'd still have a friend. now I've got a job but no friend. if I—

But I gave up. My thumbs refused to type anymore. I stared out the window for a little longer, over toward what I thought might be Broadway. I was struck by an idea. I put my plate in the sink and went upstairs.

Paul was lying on his bed wearing embarrassing purple pajamas, reading.

I sat on my bed and started pulling on a shoe.

"What're you doing?" Paul asked.

"What's it look like?"

"Well, it looks like you're going somewhere, but that can't be right, because you don't have anywhere to go."

I pulled my other shoe on.

"What're you doing, Mac?" he asked.

I looked up at him. "I'm going to shoot the test."

"What?"

"I'm shooting it."

"Are you dumb?" he asked me.

"They won't even know we're there," I said. "We're going guerrilla."

"We?"

"If you don't want to come, I'll do it alone. But if they make history tonight, I don't want to be tucked up in bed," I said, standing. "I want to be ringside."

"You have a death wish, don't you? Melody told us Gatt's after us. Why did you even put the stupid sneakers up in the first place?"

"We were gone either way," I said. "We didn't put something up, we lost our job. We put it up, we lost a friend. That's just the way it was."

"There's no way I'm coming," Paul said.

I pulled my sweater on. "Melody and Gatt hate us," I said. "Apart from the UnSneaks, we've way underdelivered for Speed and Tony, and my bet is we'll be back begging for our jobs scraping fat off the grill next week. I came here to do something big, but New York has sucked for us. This is our last chance to make it unsuck."

He knew I was right. Our life was a toilet right now. I delivered the final flush.

"If they run a perpetual motion vehicle the length of the city with no fuel whatsoever, it'll be the biggest thing since the wheel. You know it will."

"Maybe," he replied.

I started walking toward the stairs. "You coming to save the world?"

"Settle down, fart tank. You're not Ben Affleck."

"Fart tank? I asked.

"Melody's gonna kill you if she catches you."

"Yeah, she might," I said.

"And Gatt?"

"I don't even want to think about him," I said. "But if he doesn't realize how important it is to tell people about this, then he's an idiot. C'mon, let's be scary and see what happens. You know you want to."

He looked at me for a long moment.

"I'm not coming," he said.

I wasn't gonna stand around all night and plead. I was sick of him standing in my way.

"My phone's full from today," I said. "Can I use yours?"

"Whatever, dude."

I chucked my phone onto the bed and grabbed Paul's off the dresser. I got to the top of the stairs and looked back. Paul was pretending not to notice that I was going, so I went downstairs and poked my dad in the hunk of white belly sticking out of his shirt.

"Oi," I said.

He growled and turned over. The man was built like a bear, and he slept like one, too. No one in history had ever woken my dad midsleep, but that was another world-first that had to happen tonight.

"Dad!" I said, louder.

"Lemmealone."

"No," I said. "I'm going out and you've got to come with me."

He swore.

I grabbed an arm and heaved him up into a seated position, nearly pulling my shoulder out of its socket. The dude must've weighed over two hundred pounds. His eyes were still closed, his mouth open, pasty tongue hanging out.

"*Dad!*" I shouted.

"Huh?" He smacked his chops and half woke. "What?"

"I've got to go out and shoot something, and I need you."

"Yooberight," he said.

"No, I won't be all right," I said. "It's New York. At night."

"Yooavagoodtime," he said. "Don'tbelate."

Then his eyes closed again, his head tilted back, his breathing went all snorty, and he started to collapse onto me. I tried to pry myself out from under him.

Most of the time it's good having lax parents. This wasn't one of those times. Sometimes you just want your dad to worry about you or be there for you or something.

I pulled my arm out, stood up, gave him one last shove, tweaked his nose quite hard, and then headed for the door.

It was me versus the city.

I pressed the elevator button and waited. I looked through the clear glass doors into the elevator shaft and down to the lobby, twenty-four floors below. It was deserted. I checked back down the hall. Everything was dead quiet. I wondered what I was doing.

The elevator arrived and I stepped inside. I went to press the button for the first floor, and I heard a door bang. I poked my head out. There was a figure coming toward me from the end of the hall. It was Paul. I grinned as he arrived. He shook his head.

"If we make it home alive, remind me not to hang out with you anymore," he said.

Broadway

"Broadway is a rebel, a renegade," Joe Gatt said in a loud voice to the assembled crowd of Hivers, standing there in the rain. "While every other major street in this city is stuck on the grid, Broadway follows its own path, going with its gut rather than someone else's plan. It's not just a street. It's an attitude. It was a major route for Native Americans, and tonight we're going to test our creativity and ingenuity and ride it, Inwood to Battery Park. May I introduce . . . Perpetual."

They clapped, cheered, whistled.

Joe Gatt spun the rotor at the back of the machine. It was parked on the edge of the street, pointing downtown.

Nothing happened.

He spun it again. Nothing.

"Great," Paul said. "This is going to be fun."

It was dark, cold, and drizzling. Paul and I were crouched behind a Dumpster outside a Dominican supermarket called Rodrigo's. I could feel the adrenaline in my gut. Sometimes you've got to do the wrong thing to do the right thing, and I'd convinced Paul that this was the right thing. I just wasn't so sure I'd convinced myself.

On the way uptown I'd texted Speed, and he'd agreed to give us till 3:00 a.m. to upload our piece. "Not a second later." It was make-or-break time.

Gatt and the machine were standing about thirty yards from us, surrounded by the four or five Swarm members. They started buzzing around the car, preparing it under the yellow glow of the streetlamps. I could make out Heath, Dan, and Melody. And the Japanese-looking girl who I'd seen working with Gatt. There was an older guy there too. He had a thin white beard. Maybe forty-something years old. Someone's dad, I figured. Dan's? The cellulosic fuel guy? He was standing by a dark blue van.

It was 11:53 p.m. In less than ten hours' time I'd be on a plane somewhere over America. But right now we were at the top of Manhattan island, right near Baker Field, the last few hundred yards of Broadway before it sweeps over into the Bronx. A cab drove by, spraying water and splashing Perpetual.

"Sonofa . . . ," I heard Gatt say.

My eyes were fixed on Melody. Yesterday we'd had that moment at the Hive when I felt like I wanted to lean over and whatever. But now it felt like I'd never speak to her again. Our job tonight was to get the footage and stay alive. That was it.

"Keep your head down, man," Paul said. "I bet that dude does tai chi or something and he's gonna use it on us."

"We're pigs," I mumbled, not meaning to say it out loud.

"What?" Paul asked, wiping his camera screen.

I didn't reply. It poured buckets. We were getting soaked, and the camera phone was having trouble dealing with the low light and moisture.

"Every time I wipe the lens it just fogs up again," he said, rubbing it on his soaking-wet top.

Just then a cheer went up among the Swarm. I looked around the edge of the bin in time to catch Gatt climbing into the driver's seat and slamming the door. I so wished it was me riding that puppy.

Then it moved. Slowly at first, but it began to pick up speed. There was no revving of engines. No sound at all, really. Just the swoosh of tires on wet asphalt. By the time it moved past us it must've been doing twenty miles per hour, soundlessly.

A second later I spied a cab, and I scurried out and flagged it down, trying to stay out of view. As the cab slowed, I heard a sharp "Hey!" It was Melody, and it wasn't a "Hey, so good to see you." It was more of a "Hey, you scum-sucking pigs." She and Heath ran toward us as the cab pulled over. Paul and I piled in and slammed our doors. I was in front. Paul in back.

"Go, go, go," I said to the driver, and he pulled out just as

Melody and Heath got to the back of the car. Heath slammed a hand on the trunk, but we were gone.

"Where are you wanting to go? And why the hurry?" the driver asked with a heavy Indian accent. Or maybe it was Pakistani? He looked like he was about eighty.

"Straight ahead," I said. "Stay on Broadway." Up ahead, Perpetual had disappeared into the rain and haze. Behind us I saw Heath, Melody, and the others jump into the back of the van and the older dude getting into the driver's seat.

"Support vehicle," I said to Paul.

"Yeah. Awesome," he said, no expression.

"Just stay behind this wacky car thing up ahead if you can, buddy," I said to the driver. Paul and I peeled off wet jackets and sweaters.

"You know Melody's gonna call Gatt and tell him we're here," Paul said.

"Well, we'd better be invisible," I said.

Paul clicked his tongue.

Rain pummeled the roof, melding with a funky Indian track on the stereo.

"Windows are foggy. Very hot breath," the driver said, smiling and turning on the AC.

"I like the music. My mom listens to this stuff. Whereabouts are you from?" I asked.

"Yes, very good music," he said with a big smile. He had the whitest teeth I'd ever seen in my life. "I am from Bangladesh. Next to India. But been in New York sixteen years. Very good city. You can call me Bruce. Like Bruce Willis, yes?" Another big, white grin.

"Cool, Bruce," I said. "I'm Mac. He's Paul."

As Perpetual approached the intersection ahead, the light turned from red to green. Same on the next intersection. And the next.

Paul was sitting in the middle of the backseat, filming what he could.

"Not too fast, please," I said. The last thing I wanted was to be seen by Gatt. But then, we also didn't want to get caught by the support van, which was only about a hundred yards behind us.

"I can't get a picture," Paul said. "Rain's too heavy. We're gonna have to speed up to pass it, get out, get a shot of it going by, then chase it again."

The driver put his foot down and overtook Gatt. Paul and I scootched low as we went by.

"Why are you tailing these dudes?" he asked. It sounded funny hearing an eighty-year-old Bangladeshi guy say "dudes." "Are you spies?" he asked with a smile.

I liked the sound of that.

"Almost," I said. "We're coolhunters."

He looked puzzled.

"It means we sell people out," Paul explained from the

back. "We lie to people, get close to them, then film things we shouldn't film—their secrets—and put them on the Internet to entertain people."

"Shut up, man," I said to him. I wasn't in the mood for the truth.

The driver looked confused. "Doesn't sound very good."

"We're not really s'posed to do that," I said. "We just got ourselves mixed up in some stuff. That car thing behind us is a perpetual motion machine. It runs on no fuel."

"No fuel?"

"No fuel," I said. "First test-drive ever, anywhere in the world, tonight. We're filming it."

"No fuel?" he said again, then gave a big white-toother. "Where am I getting one of these? Save the world, no? Not to mention my wallet."

"So they say," I said. "This is good here. Could you just pull onto this street on the right? We'll jump out."

"How long you will be?" Bruce asked. "Where will you go after?"

"We'll be five minutes," I said. "We're going to the other end of Broadway. How much will that cost?"

The driver gave a long, low whistle as he pulled into the side street.

"You rich?" he asked.

"Not very," I said, though Paul and I had hardly spent any of our expense allowance for the week.

"I look after you," he said. "I wait here. Not often I have spies on board."

Paul and I jumped out of the cab and ran across the road to near the Inwood–207th Street subway station. We scuttled under an awning and waited. Paul set up the camera on the edge of a garbage bin to keep the shot steady, and we got down low, out of sight. Cars whooshed by in the wet, headlights blinding us. It was hard to see where Perpetual was. I was thinking that maybe it had broken down. But then it appeared on the phone screen. Only one headlight, and it was slower than the other traffic, in the lane closest to us. It looked like a spaceship cruising by, making no sound, illuminated for a moment by the streetlights near the station and then gone again. The van was right behind it. Paul and I crouched way out of sight.

We jumped back into the cab and told Bruce to put pedal to metal. We stayed low as we passed Perpetual, then we jumped out around 192nd Street. We hopped in and out of the cab for the next half hour or so—cruising ahead, diving out, shooting, trying to get a fresh angle or a different shot size each time. There were some deeply sketchy characters on the streets at that time of night. I was glad Paul had come. Not that he could do much, but at least I wouldn't die alone.

Broadway cut through Trinity Cemetery, where Bruce said a bunch of famous dead people were laid to rest. Then down through Harlem, which he said was home to what he reckoned was his favorite restaurant in the city, Sylvia's. "Good grits," he said.

Perpetual charged through the night, streetlights changing right on cue, taxi meter climbing above eighty dollars, but Bruiser insisted he'd take care of us. "I am a coolhunter now," he said, flashing those pearly whites.

He pointed out Dr. Martin Luther King Jr. Boulevard and a tree-lined section of Broadway where Columbia University was. He said four American presidents had studied there.

The rain had begun to ease, and just before 1:00 a.m., Paul's mom called while he was filming out the cab window. The ring tone wrecked the shot. Paul tried to sound sleepy.

"Hi," he croaked.

"Paul? Are you awake? I thought I'd leave a message to wish you luck on the flight." Her voice was so loud it was like she was sitting there in the cab with us. For a second I almost wished she was.

"Yeah, no. I was sleeping."

"Well, it sounds very noisy. Where are you sleeping? On the street?" she said. "I can hear a car."

"We've just got the window open," he said.

"In a highrise? They don't let you open windows in high-rises."

"Sorry, Mom, you're cutting out."

"I want to know why you're not in bed at this hour," she said.

"Hello? Are you there?" Paul asked, then he hit end and switched his phone to the meeting setting.

"It's for her own good," he said. "She needs to be protected from the truth at all times."

Not long after, we hit Times Square, where Seventh Avenue collides with Broadway to create one of the busiest intersections in the world. Even after 1:00 a.m. on a regular Monday night in March, the place was pumping. Paul and I stepped out of the cab, gazing all around. Giant TV screens exploded with new-car ads. Restaurants, people, taxis, theaters everywhere. Massive billboards with hot models in their undies, stretching way up into the sky. It was a real brain bang.

"We've got to be out there," I said to Paul, pointing to a traffic island in the middle of the manic intersection.

"There's no place to hide," Paul said.

"I know, but this is the money shot, and I want to be in among it. We get this shot and we go home, okay?"

"For real?" he said.

"For real."

"Giddyup."

We crossed the street to the traffic island and set up the shot. If I'd stretched my arms I could have almost touched the cars whipping by on both sides. Paul was right. There was nothing for us to hide behind, but it looked spectacular: blasts of color from big-screen TVs, and motion blur as traffic tore past the lens.

A few minutes later we saw Perpetual about to come through the intersection. I started recording as cars poured down Broadway. I got a nice wide shot with all the lights of the square, and then I zoomed in for a tighter shot of Perpetual. I could see Gatt through all the lights flickering off the curved fighter jet window in front of him.

He was in the closest lane, which meant that I could get an in-your-face, front-on shot with Perpetual driving directly toward us. When he was about three cars away, I got down low and leaned as close to the traffic as I could without getting cleaned up. I could feel the rush of air from cars whooshing past as Perpetual appeared from behind a red SUV. It looked like it was coming directly into the lens. Definitely the shot of the night. But, get this. As Gatt went by, he saw me. He turned his head and looked right at us. Then he stared over his shoulder at us as he zoomed by.

"Did you see that?" Paul asked.

"Yeah," I said, cold adrenaline racing from my heart to my fingers and face. "But what's he gonna do? Stop? He's stuck in a perpetual motion car. We're done. Let's go upload."

We watched as Perpetual disappeared into the traffic.

"I wish we could see if he made it all the way," Paul said.

I pocketed Paul's phone, and we waited at the crosswalk, ready to head back to Bruce, who was idling on a side street just off Times Square. That's when a dark blue van pulled up and Heath, Dan, and Melody appeared from the sliding side door. Cars behind beeped at the van, but it didn't move. The three of them began squeezing through the crowd of pedestrians on the packed traffic island, heading toward us.

I could hear the wail of a distant siren as Paul and I started to back up.

"What do we do?" Paul asked, panicked.

"We run," I said.

← Coolhunting → Sucks

A bus slammed on its brakes and just missed us as Paul and I weaved through traffic to the far side of Times Square, a long, long way from where Bruce was waiting for us in our cab. The traffic was too nuts to get back to him now.

Once we hit the sidewalk, we bolted down Broadway and ducked onto a street on our right. I had no idea where it led, but I figured Heath, Dan, and Melody would give up quickly.

I was wrong.

We ran past a bank and a big theater. We crossed the street as the blue van rounded the corner.

"That's them," I said to Paul.

"What?"

The van was speeding down the street toward us. Paul and I slipped into the mouth of an alley to our left. I ran into a guy as I rounded the corner, then looked down the alley. It ran for fifty yards and it was a dead end, so I U-turned back onto the street. Paul was on my heels. I looked over my shoulder, and the van was about forty yards back, stuck behind a street cleaner.

"C'mon!" I said, having flashbacks of the skateboarders on the empty block, the last shady situation I'd gotten us into. We ran past a bagel shop and a coffee house, and then I saw a tiny Italian restaurant with red-and-white-checked curtains and an OPEN sign in the window. I pulled the heavy wood door open and we slipped inside. There was one customer sitting at a booth with a tablecloth that matched the curtains.

"We've got to stop," Paul said.

The van pulled up outside, and I started moving through the restaurant.

"Mac, stop," Paul hissed.

"How can I help you?" a tired, old waiter with a thick gray mustache asked. He was standing there folding napkins.

"Do you have a back door?" I asked.

"We do in the kitchen, but I'm afraid—"

I was gone. Paul followed. We moved quickly past the lone diner as I heard the front door of the restaurant squeal open. We pushed through saloon doors into the kitchen, which was empty. It looked pretty dirty back there. I was glad we weren't eating. Then I shoved open the rear door and we fell out into a narrow, seedy-looking backstreet. There was a dude in a hooded jacket sitting with his back against the wall, head down. I didn't know which way to run.

"We're so gonna die out here," Paul said.

I decided to head up the lane beside the restaurant and back onto the street. Just then, Melody emerged from the front door of the Italian place and called out, "Mac!" I didn't stop, so she jumped into the van and it started tracking us again.

"What are we running from?" Paul screamed at me.

"From them," I said. "They'll take the footage."

"So what!"

Up ahead was a cross street. We took a left and ran past money changers, a cheap hotel, a group of shady dudes hanging out on some steps. One of them threw a can at us. It missed, clattering across the sidewalk and under a parked car.

Halfway down the block, the van was still moving steadily down the street behind us. They weren't giving in. My throat was dry, my eyes were hot, and I was starting to freak. *Maybe I do need to stop,* I thought. But I was still embarrassed by what I'd done to Melody, I was scared of what they might do to us, and, truth was, I still wanted to "win" the coolhunt.

I heard Paul yelp, and I turned just in time to see him collapse onto the wet sidewalk and roll. I'd swear I actually heard skin grating off his hands. He'd kneecapped himself on a fire hydrant. I stopped and ran back.

"You okay?" I said, reaching for him. He grabbed my hand, and I pulled him up off the sidewalk. I flicked a look toward the van and realized that it was only about four car lengths away. We were gone.

But if I knew one thing, I knew I was a survivor. I could

think fast and turn things around. I'd done it plenty of times in life-or-death situations with our inventions. As we staggered along, Paul leaning on my shoulder for support, van closing in, my mind sprinted ahead of us, finding a way.

I took the next left, and I could see the lights of Times Square up ahead again. We'd almost circled the block. I figured if we made it back to Times Square we could get lost in the crowd. The street we were on was busier, brighter, too, which felt good.

Paul was slowing, grabbing his hip, limping badly.

"You've got to stand up, man."

"Stitch," he said.

I wanted to scream at him, but I sucked it in. I looked around and saw the van take the corner. I grabbed Paul by the shirt and dragged him into a souvenir shop—bright white fluorescent lights, I Heart NY stuff everywhere. An old, white-haired woman was at the counter with a pair of "NY" hearts on springs sticking out like antennae from a red headband.

"Good evening. Or good morning. Late night, boys?" she asked.

Paul and I didn't respond. I ducked in behind a postcard stand. Paul flopped onto the floor behind some low shelves filled with plush polar bears holding "NY" hearts. I peered out through the front window just in time to see the van appear. The driver—the older guy with the beard—had his window down. He was scanning around, hunting for us. At one stage he seemed to look right at me, and the van stopped.

"It's all over," I whispered to Paul.

But then he turned away and the van kept moving, and a second later it was gone.

I covered my face with my hand.

"What you hidin' from?" the lady asked.

I thought about it for a moment. "I don't know," I said.

I slumped onto the shop floor beside Paul. I could barely get a lungful of air. Paul had his chin on his chest. His cheeks were flaming red. He'd never run so far or fast in his life. He usually avoided exercise at all costs. He peeled up his jeans and checked out his knee.

"You boys like some water?" the woman said, heart antennae bouncing around on top of her head.

I nodded. "Please."

A minute later she returned, and we sat there guzzling skanky tap water, surrounded by thousands of nasty New York souvenirs—bears, key rings, coasters, snow globes, and giant pencils—under way-too-bright fluorescent lights.

Is this it? I wondered. Was this the end of the line for us? Was this seriously how New York was going to end?

Paul groaned. "Coolhunting sucks."

He was so right.

We thanked the woman for our sewer water.

"How much for a pair of the springy New York antennae?"

I asked her. I figured we owed her something, and they were the ugliest thing in there. Which was saying something.

"Four ninety-five," she said.

I threw a five onto the counter and grabbed my antennae, and we headed outside.

I half-expected the van to pull up and dudes to bundle us inside, tape our mouths, and make us disappear without a trace.

But that didn't happen. My legs were jelly. We walked back along puddled streets toward Times Square, feeling very ordinary. When we made it back there, we headed to where we'd left Bruce, the taxi driver, even though we figured he wouldn't be there.

But he was. Just sitting in the driver's seat, reading a newspaper and picking his nose. I pulled open the passenger door.

"You two boys okay?" he asked.

"Why didn't you leave?" I said.

"You owe me too much money," he said with a smile. "And I knew you would come back. You are good boys. Where did you go?"

Paul jumped into the backseat, shut the door, closed his eyes. I jumped into the front.

"Just around the block," I said.

"And where to now?" he asked.

"Home. Lower East Side. The Ludlow," I said.

As Bruiser pulled out into traffic, I took out the phone and looked back at some of what we'd shot. It was 1:52 a.m. We had an hour to edit and upload Perpetual to the site.

The footage looked hot. Speed and the Coolhunters sub-scribers would flip over it. It was a world-first, it had an enviro edge, it was shot on location in New York City. It had it all. We might as well have booked our tickets to Shanghai that night.

By first light we'd be heroes. I'd have "made it" in New York City.

So why did I feel so bad?

Face-Off

Gatt slammed my face against the back of Perpetual, warm skin on cold metal. Heath grabbed Paul by the back of the neck and ground his head into the silver chassis, next to mine. I was starting to think our trip downtown to straighten things out wasn't such a hot idea.

We'd made it back to the hotel fifty-three minutes before our 3:00 a.m. deadline. All we had to do was cut the footage and upload it. But I couldn't do it. Not till I'd sorted things out with Melody and Gatt. I'd told Bruiser to turn around, to go back to Broadway, to find them. I'd figured things couldn't get much worse.

Again I'd figured wrong.

We found the perpetual motion machine broken down on the side of the street, a block from where my dad had stalled the car on our first night in town. We'd pulled up on the north side of Canal, a cross street, just in time to see Gatt get out of the vehicle and give the side of Perpetual an almighty kick. I'd asked Bruce to wait for us in the cab. I said things might get a little gnarly.

"What do I do with you?" Gatt asked. He was leaning over my shoulder, inches from my face. I thought about answering with something smart, but I figured now probably wasn't the time. I could feel his hot breath on me. It was rank. I was maybe seconds away from getting whacked, and all I could think about was his fish breath. Maybe he'd stopped in for sushi someplace along the way?

The side of my head was pressed against Perpetual, forcing me to look at Melody, standing beside the car. She looked back, no expression. She wasn't about to save me.

"You can have the footage," I said to Gatt. "We'll give it to you. That was the plan. We wanted to sh—"

"Shut up," he said. "Tell me how you knew about tonight."

I looked at Melody. Her eyes widened, threatening.

"I overheard," I said. "That day we were around. Sunday."

"You heard the time *and* the place?" he asked.

"Yeah," I croaked.

"And my girl Melody had nothing to do with it?"

Melody and I locked eyes. Cars swished by. This was my chance if I wanted to take her down. Things did not look good for me and Paul. Pinning it on her might make it possible for us to get out of this alive. I had to make a good decision. I looked right inside her, and I knew what I had to do.

"No," I said. "It was just me. I overheard someone. I don't remember who."

Melody's shoulders dropped, and she looked away.

"Give me what you shot," he said.

I squeezed my hand into my jeans pocket, popped the memory stick out of Paul's phone, and handed it to Gatt, who threw it on the wet pavement. I immediately regretted giving it to him. I thought he was about to grind it into oblivion, when Melody spoke.

"I showed them," she said.

Gatt stopped. "Excuse me?"

"I showed them the machine," she said, eyes glistening.

"No she didn't," I said, my jaw numb from the cold. A stiff wind blew up Broadway. The huddled group drew their jackets around themselves. Dan and the Japanese chick from the Hive were there too, looking on.

"Yes I did," she said. "We were going to show you the footage, let you decide. They promised not to do anything with it unless you said so. And they haven't done anything with it. It means something, Joe, what you've done. I know you don't create things for anybody else, but—"

"That's right. I don't," he said.

"But this is bigger than you," she said. "Stop being so stubborn, and just have a look at the video."

"The machine doesn't work," he said.

"Yes it does," Melody said. "It's just—"

"Am I driving it right now?" he asked, almost daring her to answer him. She didn't, for a few seconds.

"No," she said eventually.

"That's because it doesn't *work*," he said, slamming his hand down on Perpetual right next to my face, leaving a dent. "So let me decide if it's important that people know about it or not."

There was silence.

A car tore by, and a guy yelled out the window at us and laughed.

"I said that it was on your head if these guys screwed up, didn't I?" Gatt asked.

"Yes," she said.

"Don't come back to Inwood," he told her, and my heart fell into my stomach. Then he turned his eyes back to me. He let go of me, and I stood up straight, turning my head from side to side, cracking my neck. Heath let go of Paul, too.

"Pick up the stick," he said to me, like I was a dog.

I looked at him for a second, then bent down and picked up the memory stick.

"Now put it back in the phone," he said.

Was he going to let us go? He was such a random dude, who'd know? I pulled the phone out of my pocket and pushed the memory card into the slot.

Gatt popped the rear hood of Perpetual, exposing the engine.

"Start recording," he said.

I swallowed hard, switched to camera mode, and pressed start. The time code ticked over.

"You won't want to miss this," he said into the lens. Then he calmly reached in and grabbed the rotor with the magnets on it, ripped it out of the machine, and tossed it to the ground. Magnets scattered.

"You get that?" he said.

"Don't," Melody said.

He then reached in and tore out a wire coil. I wanted to stop filming, but I was scared.

The old guy in the support vehicle opened his door to see what was going on. I looked back, and Bruiser was standing beside his cab. The other Hivers looked on, too freaked to say anything. Paul looked devastated. My eyes flicked back to the phone screen as Gatt ripped a thick piece of metal pipe out from under the engine. He raised it above his head and then brought it down, smashing the engine, denting and busting up the remaining parts.

"Get a good angle?" he said to me when he was done. I hit stop and lowered the phone. He was breathing heavy, muscles pumped. He'd annihilated his creation in front of the people who had helped him build it. We all stood there, silently waiting for him to go nuts again.

"Now give it to me," he said.

I popped the card out and slowly raised it, offering it to

him. It was everything we'd risked our lives for—a tiny piece of plastic sticking out from between my shaking fingers. He took it and looked at it for a second in his palm, deciding what to do with it. He smiled to himself, and I tried to force a smile too.

Then he tossed the card down again, mashing it into the road with his sneakered foot. Within three seconds, any evidence that Joe Gatt had built the world's first fully functioning fuel-free vehicle was gone.

"I can't be bought," he said. Then he dropped the hunk of metal he'd been using to destroy the machine, turned, and stepped out into the street. He walked right into the center of the street. Two cars swerved to miss him.

"Joe!" Melody said, but he didn't listen. She waited for a tow truck to pass, then started to cross the road. Without turning around, he shouted, "Leave me alone." Cars came down the street and were forced to veer around him, honking, but he didn't care. It was like he couldn't see them. Gatt just looked straight ahead and walked off into the darkness of Broadway, New York's main vein—a rebel, a renegade.

Epilogue:
Somewhere over America

⟶

"Sleep is so rock 'n' roll right now. Sleep is the new awake. By the end of this year they're gonna be sleepin' in malls in Oklahoma."

I was watching our Sleepers piece on my phone as we flew over America. It was streaming live off the Coolhunters site, and it was going off! Ninety-six thousand views in eight hours, and counting. Our biggest piece ever. At 2:52 a.m., when we got back to the hotel, Paul and I had decided to upload it. As the vid ended I flicked to my blog page and started flowing. My thumbs were getting faster.

> hey
>
> is it our fault that gatt did what he did or would he have done
>
> it anyway? was that really the end of perpetual or was it just a

bad night? i dont know but i feel like in the end we did the right thing. we went downtown n faced the dude. offered 2 show him the footage. we apol'd 2 melody + thanked her for saving our lives. gave her a ride home. but i still dont know what 2 make of gatt. @ some point in the trip i thought i wanted 2 be him. the dude knows what he believes in. rock solid. like my folks. maybe thats what annoyed me about him. theyre always telling me to b true 2 myself n go with my gut but truth is that sometimes i dont know what i really want or who i am or what my gut is saying and sometimes i mess up. and is gatt a better person than me because hes so hard-core on staying true 2 himself that he destroys what he creates?

My phone beeped with a message. It was Speed:

U guys rock! Yr Sleepers piece has the 2nd highest hit numbers on site this week. Sleep is about to have its iPod moment. It's going to go large, lads. In fact I'm going 4 a nap right now. I knew I made the right decision on u guys. Never doubted u. Can't wait 2 c what u dig up back in Kings Bay. Make sure it's as hot as the Sleepers. C u in Shanghai in 3 months' time. Oh, and nobody loses thr job. For now.
S

Without thinking, I tried to pass the phone to Paul. He didn't take it. I looked up at him. He was asleep. My mom's herbal anti-freak-out drops had worked. He still had fresh sweat on his top lip, and his hands had a pretty good grip on the vinyl armrests, but he was asleep.

I looked across to my dad. Sleeping, too. His beard and hair were chaos, Greenpeace T-shirt stained and torn. The guy never changed. I'd been through all this crazy stuff in New York, and he was still just the same old Dad. *So* not New York. But maybe that was okay. I mean, he seemed to know that sleep was hot way before New York realized it. He's been sleeping twelve hours a day for years. Maybe I needed to look to him to find the next big thing from now on. I mean, maybe snoring, blackheads, and yellow teeth were about to take off?

I pulled my New York springy-antennae-hearts headband out of my seatback, stuck it on my head, closed my eyes, and tried to sleep. But I couldn't. My head was jammed with thousands of snapshot flashes of our trip.

I love where I'm from but, to me, if you're gonna go anywhere, you go to New York. Even to smell the place. That's just the way it is.